I0543516

TRICK

or

TRY ME

Justice Willoughby

All rights reserved
Copyright ©2025 Justice Willoughby

This is a work of fiction. The names, characters and places depicted are either invented by the author or used fictitiously. Any resemblance to real persons, events and places is purely coincidental. No part of this book may be reproduced in any form or by any means, electronic, mechanical, photocopying, microfilm, recording or otherwise without the written permission of the publisher.

CHAPTER 1

Markus

The motorway towards Salem Falls is lined with fiery-hued trees. Countless copper-toned leaves lift as I pass, swept by a humid wind that signals rain. It's a sight that captivates me again after so long.

It's been almost ten years since I last drove this road in Massachusetts, yet every bend feels increasingly familiar, as if no time has gone by.

Maybe it's just an illusion, one that Salem Falls and New England can create all too easily. Everything here is steeped in memories, at least for me, or magic, depending on how you want to call this feeling that is gripping me more and more intensely as I approach my destination.

I almost furiously turn off the radio when the music is interrupted to make way for local news, and "Salem Falls Halloween Fair" is mentioned. It almost feels like a slight aimed directly at me, but then again... what could I expect? I know the programme by heart since I'm also involved in it, with its stalls, fun games and challenges, shows, lectures, and themed presentations, including some creative writing workshops I've agreed to take part in as a "teacher". Or rather, my publisher has guaranteed my presence, to be more precise.

In any case, it's during some of these conferences and presentations that I'll have to discuss my latest book, *The Black Shadows of Vengeance*, a novel about "ghosts" who return from the past with less than peaceful intentions. Markus Leigh's latest release, another guaranteed success!

I smile bitterly. Maybe I am too, a ghost from the past. And the fact that I agreed to present my book here only confirms that. I acted on impulse when my publisher suggested it; I realise that. And I never act on impulse; for the last ten years, my entire life has been meticulously planned. Especially when it comes to my work. It's the only thing I consider truly important now. Everything else... no, better not think about it!

I try to zone out and think about other things. Specifically, I review the main topics of my presentation that have been agreed upon. I like to have an outline of the topics that will be covered so I don't feel unprepared. I haven't met the person who will introduce me yet, but I hate being caught off guard.

I realise I've reached my destination even before the GPS indicates I'm entering the town. In fact, I shouldn't have needed it at all. As I wind through the streets leading to the centre, I'm greeted by the same unmistakable mix of scents, both penetrating and comforting: melted wax, cinnamon, wet leaves, wood. Salem Falls remains a town that relies on atmosphere and charm, and October can be seen as its sacred month. The month when everything here seems to shine anew. I steal a glance at the colonial houses, decorated with lanterns, pumpkins, and scarecrows; the windows and shopfronts overflow with painted pumpkins, witches and monsters of various kinds, and red and black candles.

Every detail takes me back to a time when I believed I'd have everything I could ever want, that it would be granted to me because, deep down, I genuinely deserved it. Now... well, now that I actually have so much more than I did back then, I'm no longer so sure.

I park in front of "Salem Falls Shelter", the small hotel my zealous publisher booked for me, where I'll be staying during my visit. Although I think two weeks is far too long. The hotel is also themed, of course. As soon as I step out of the car, I notice the cold air slicing through my skin like a razor. I lift my scarf slightly to better cover my neck and part of my face, but meanwhile I inhale deeply. The smell of the sea isn't far off, mingling with the humidity of the evening that will soon grow darker.

I ascend the stairs, pass through the entrance, and glance around, feeling a little disoriented. It looks welcoming; it must be fairly new, as it wasn't here before. That's just as well, at least I won't have any memories of this place. I walk up to the reception desk, ready to say hello and introduce myself with my usual look of a wild yet charming young man. Everyone likes me, both men and women, I know that, and I don't mind at all. In fact, I'm not opposed to having adventures whenever the chance arises.

The girl at the counter, a blonde in her twenties, widens her eyes and hands me the key with a dazzling smile and a captivated expression. Okay, she recognised me. So I won't need to introduce myself.

'Markus Leigh, I can't believe it!' she exclaims, clasping her hands together and biting her red-lined lips. 'I mean, I knew you were coming; we were waiting for you. I've read all your books, I mean, almost all of them... *Steps into the Dark Soul* is my absolute favourite. It kept me awake at night. I couldn't sleep for days!'

'I'm sorry… about the sleepless nights, I mean!'

I smile and wink at her. I'm used to this kind of reaction. I'm used to much more, to be honest. The girl is holding back from the enthusiasm of some fans.

'Oh, but it was worth it!' she giggles as I see her blush and she runs a hand through her blonde hair. 'Anyway, it's a pleasure to welcome you here. I had my shift changed specifically, knowing you were coming today... I'm Allie. I'm available for anything you need...'

She bites her full lips. There, exactly. Correction, she's not holding back.

I don't disdain female attention, even though I usually prefer men. I avoid mentioning it, though.

'Thanks, Allie. I'll keep that in mind.'

'You're welcome, Markus. I am here.'

I tilt my head and smile. Honestly, I just want to rest right now. Maybe I'll go to my room and spend some time studying the programme more carefully. Thinking back, just before I left, Nevil Larsen, my publisher, rang me to say there would be some minor changes and that he'd send me an update via email as soon as he could.

'Do you happen to have a detailed schedule of events and presentations, Allie?'

'Yes, of course! They've just delivered.' She nods and smiles again, appearing happy to be of service and to spend time with me. But then her gaze darkens and her smile fades. 'There have been some changes to the previous schedule. Unfortunately, "Salem Falls Tea Room", where you were supposed to give your main presentation, has a plumbing problem that caused flooding. It won't be ready in time. It's a real shame, our tea room is really famous in the area!'

'Yes… I know it, I'm truly sorry!'

'However, the "Salem Falls Halloween Fair" board of events quickly found a suitable solution,' she sighs and hands me one of the flyers, retrieving it from under the counter. 'The presentation has been moved to "Moonlight Café & Bookshop". It's a new venue, less well-known, but it's still a wonderful place; I'm sure you'll love it.'

"Moonlight". Allie, clearly, can't know that. But I'm absolutely sure I'll like it because I know it all too well. Even if it wasn't planned. Even if, in part, it makes my blood run cold thinking about it. Even if it didn't exist yet when I left.

Meanwhile, inevitably, the thought takes up more and more space in my mind. Of course, "Moonlight Café & Bookshop" — the place where everything began. Or, if not everything, then a significant part. The dream place that only existed in my imagination. And then... and then him.

Caleb Monroe. I still remember the night he told me about his dream of opening his own shop, a haven for those who love books and coffee. Just the way he would have liked it, the place he would have loved to retreat to if such a place existed. When he thought of the name, he said he would call it exactly that, "Moonlight", a simple name, perhaps banal and unoriginal. Because moonlight, unlike sunlight, never blinds. It's soft, welcoming, and unobtrusive. And he, in the moonlight, could recognise himself. He felt at home, as he had always felt at home in Salem Falls, where he had taken refuge after his college years.

I thought it remained just a dream, just as we were. The truth is, I never investigated, I never tried to find out. I preferred to walk away and archive everything. But at the same time, I have no doubts. I know that "Moonlight" can only be his.

'Mr. Leigh...?' Allie must be sensing my sudden disorientation and calling me back to the present. 'Is everything okay?'

'Yes, of course. I just need to rest a bit,' I smile again, appearing casual and seductive, as expected of me. 'Thanks, Allie.'

'I can call one of the guys to help you with your luggage and...' She places a hand on her forehead. 'How silly of me, you must be used to big city hotels! But we've reserved one of our best rooms for you.'

'No, don't worry.' I smile again, gripping the key in one hand and my luggage in the other. 'Really, I prefer it this way. Hotels in big cities are incredibly dull.'

Finally, I walk away and head for the stairs to my room. I feel disoriented and have a lump in my throat, but at least I'm no longer forced to pretend or act a part.

I reach the second floor; the hallway smells of wood and vanilla candles. I enter my room, leave my suitcase at the entrance, and flop onto the bed, staring at the ceiling. I'm here now, and I can't help but continue with the project. But the truth is, everything inside me rebels at the thought of seeing him again. I don't feel at all prepared, that's all!

And yet, damn it, I asked for it! I could have refused, gone elsewhere, or stayed in New York to rest after my umpteenth effort and prepare for the international tour scheduled for next year. But I didn't. Because the truth is, a deeper, more secret part of me wants nothing more—and it knew full well that the possibility of seeing him again was

12

real. The other part, however, the more rational one, had convinced me that I had closed that chapter forever.

Perhaps I returned here not for the Halloween festival, nor for the conferences, workshops, and the presentation of my new book, but to discover if, amidst the many shadows of my past, there is still a flicker of light, though fragile, almost insubstantial.

To come to terms with my past, in short.

I manage to rest a bit and order dinner at the hotel restaurant. Afterwards, I decide to take a stroll and set off through the town streets. The streets of Salem Falls, during the third week of October, are a maze of flickering lights, which I know quite well. There are all kinds of people out and about: families, tourists, young people in bathing suits. Every face I encounter reflects a fragment of a life that has long since passed away. Despite everything, I lose myself among the candy stalls and the scent of mulled cider until I find myself in front of a lit shop window. Even without meaning to, my steps have led me here.

At the top, there is a polished brass plaque that reads: "Moonlight Café & Bookshop".

My heart starts pounding, as if I've been running, but I take a few steps closer. Behind the glass, amid the shelves overflowing with books and a few cups of coffee, I catch a glimpse of a familiar profile. Immediately after, dark blond hair pushed back with his hand, broad shoulders, a sweet yet provocative smile.

Caleb.

I can't go inside. Not now, not like this. Not tonight.

So I stand still on the pavement, unable to take my eyes off him, his confident movements, in an environment he loves and knows well.

Caleb Monroe remains true to himself. Always present, exactly where he decided to stay. Because Salem Falls never forgets.

And neither do I.

CHAPTER 2

Caleb

I close the register and turn off almost half the lights in the room. It's late now, yet "Moonlight" is still filled with that typical pre-Halloween energy, along with the smell of roasted pumpkins, the warm lighting, and the sound of the light rain tapping against the windows.

I cherish this part of the evening when everything seems to slow down, and I can finally be alone with my thoughts, which always take over these days, stealing much of the relief and peace I believe I truly deserve.

But unfortunately, these autumn days are once again becoming difficult for me, leading me to retreat into the past.

Ten years have gone by. Ten cursed, long years since Markus Leigh decided to seek his fortune elsewhere, where he could truly give his career a proper boost. Yes, because his career mattered more than us, more than our relationship we fought for. Which, truth be told, we were still fighting for.

Sometimes I deceive myself into thinking I have forgotten him, once and for all. But this season, unfortunately, always draws me back to him. That's why I dislike it and try not to involve myself in anything, especially the events that regularly happen in Salem Falls, like the Halloween festival. I just wait for it all to be over and for the Christmas preparations to start in November.

I also try to avoid anything related to him and his success as much as possible. But then I stumble upon his name, see his image on some magazine or cover, and realise that Markus Leigh has never really left. Not from my mind, at least. Not from my heart.

He's still there, beneath my skin, like a scar that burns when the weather changes. Maybe that's also why, in the end, I decided to turn my dream into reality and build this place: to fill the void he left me with something truly mine. Something that won't abandon me.

Books and coffee, words and aromas: a delicate balance, but one that holds together the pieces of my heart, managing to reconcile me with myself and with the world.

'If it's okay with you, I'm heading off, boss!' Chelsea Davenport, my lively young employee, smiles at me as she wraps her orange scarf around her neck. 'Just a reminder that in two days, the place will be packed for the presentation of the new book by the "surprise" author invited to the festival. "Salem Falls Tea Room" isn't usable, so the organisers have asked us to make a last-minute change of plans. We'll just have to make the room available, and they'll handle the refreshments, book signings, and everything else. We don't have any of his books at the moment, but we should order them in the next few days since he's supposed to stay until Halloween! Anyway, I hope they'll bring us the final posters tomorrow morning.'

'Yes, of course. It'll be excellent publicity for us.'

I greet her words with a mix of annoyance and indifference. I don't usually behave this way, but Chelsea knows me by now and knows I'm allergic to this time of year; so, since I don't want to hear about it, she handles the events and presentations for "Salem Falls Halloween Fair". I know she enjoys this responsibility, so our teamwork works well for both of us. October is her month, after all.

'Absolutely! And he's really... wow!'

I shake my head and roll my eyes. For Chelsea, nearly everyone is "wow", so I don't expect anything special.

'You must be exaggerating, as usual.'

'No, this time I'm not exaggerating at all!'

'Okay, you've piqued my curiosity.' More than anything, I know she can't wait to tell me, so I oblige. 'Who is it this time?'

'Hold on tight, boss: Markus Leigh!' She clasps her hands together and entwines her fingers. 'I don't know if you know him... he's really attractive! And he's the one who writes those slightly macabre horror novels and psychological thrillers that your Aunt Leanne loves so much. You know him, right?'

I know him, unfortunately. But I had always avoided him until now; I didn't expect him to agree to present his new book here. Besides, it's not even the first time they have invited him, as they often referred to him as a local celebrity, especially in past years, during the early part of his career, when they still remembered him living here for a while.

The name cuts me like a blade, once more. I am well aware of Aunt Leanne's enthusiasm for him. For ten years, she has been collecting his books, ordering them on Amazon, and everything associated with him, just as she always does with her favourite author, Stephen King. The fact that he lived here and had a kind of "special friendship", as she calls it, with me, only deepens her respect for Markus.

Chelsea's green eyes, fixed on me, compel me to respond and reconnect with the present reality. I try not to reveal my emotions, to keep my tone neutral and indifferent, but my voice emerges hoarse and slightly strangled.

'Yes, I know him. But he's not really my thing.'

'Hmm... too bad! You prefer adventures like Wilbur Smith, don't you?'

'Yes, exactly!' I nod confidently, without offering any further details.

The truth is, I like everything, really everything. I enjoy any genre if I come across a good story. But not Markus Leigh. Never Markus Leigh.

As soon as Chelsea leaves, I find myself standing behind the counter, my fingers clenched around a not-too-warm cup of coffee. I huff and stare at "Moonlight"'s front door as if it might burst open at any moment.

The thought of Markus returning to Salem Falls —and right here, to my coffee shop —makes my stomach turn. I've even lost my appetite for tonight. I'm not sure if it's because of the anger I still feel towards him, or something worse I don't even want to think about.

Damn, all we needed was him! For him to actually come back here, in person. It wasn't enough to have Aunt Leanne with her monthly book clubs in the private room at "Moonlight", and the customers who, from time to time, come looking for his books that Chelsea and I are forced to order online for them.

Perhaps the real "problem" is that I never had a proper ending with him. Just a letter, a sudden goodbye, then an all-too-brief email, and finally, as far as I'm concerned, a separation that no one since him has managed to bridge. Like a scratch in my heart that has never healed.

I close the shop, switch off the lights completely, and head upstairs where I live. From my apartment balcony, I can see historic downtown Salem Falls: lanterns, costumes, pumpkins, and the reflection of candles in the darkness.

I sigh and run a hand through my hair. I genuinely don't know how I'll manage tomorrow and the days that follow. Perhaps I should fake a terrible flu, stay locked away here, and leave everything to Chelsea for a week. Or even two. Until he goes, basically. But I know that wouldn't be fair. I can't run from problems like a coward.

I keep my gaze fixed on downtown Salem Falls. I almost feel as if the wind carries the echo of a distant voice, the ringing of bells. But it's nothing truly magical; perhaps it's just the old and sad "Calloway Theatre". After many years of splendour, thanks to Julia Calloway's work, the local theatre has sadly been abandoned for several years. But sometimes, especially during this time of year, "Salem Falls Halloween Fair" still uses its exterior for some supernatural-themed events.

I decide to go back, feeling suddenly distressed and exhausted. I reach my room, sit on the bed, and take a tin box from the bedside table drawer. It's been there, even though I haven't opened it in years. I persuade myself to do so now, as if driven by an irresistible impulse. Inside, among other small mementoes of our relationship, I find a photograph. It's Markus and me, then in our early twenties, sitting on the wall in front of "Calloway Theatre", where we kissed for the first time. He was laughing, the sun shining on his eyes and his thick dark hair.

I wonder whether seeing him again will make me feel better or only bring more torment. Perhaps both. Some wounds never fully heal; you just learn to live with the pain, as I have with the tragedies life has thrown at me. Yet, at the same time, maybe I could finally give our relationship some clear closure. It would be a step forward for me.

I put the photograph back in the box and then at the bottom of the drawer. I head to the kitchen, grab a beer from the fridge, and then move to the living room. I sip from the bottle as I stand in front of the window, watching the rain gradually intensify.

Suddenly, I think I hear a noise; I'm almost sure it's just the wind, but I'd rather go downstairs and check. I move cautiously down the stairs, feeling a sensation that's overtaking me, absorbing my thoughts until it sends a shiver down my spine.

I reach my place and stand in the doorway leading upstairs. I look around; "Moonlight" is shrouded in darkness. It was all just my imagination. I shake my head and prepare to go back upstairs. But just as I'm about to turn around, I quickly glance at the window.

Am I fooling myself? Is this really just my imagination?

Because the alternative would be... No, that figure standing in the rain outside the window can't be him. I can see his dark coat, his hands in his pockets, and his scarf around his neck. His head is slightly tilted, but his gaze remains fixed inside the shop.

My heart starts racing almost too quickly. I'm not imagining it; I recognise his physique, his features. It's truly him!

Markus.

I stand still, watching him, knowing that in the dark place where I stand, he won't be able to see me. I feel suspended, as if time has suddenly stopped.

I could move from here, go open the door, face him. Seize the moment and shout at him everything I've held back inside for so many years.

But I don't; I freeze. I just stand there, watching him, studying his figure and features until he decides to look away and start walking. Then he vanishes from my sight completely.

I close my eyes for a moment, sigh, and angrily push back the lock of hair that has fallen over my eyes. A part of me always knew that, deep down, it wasn't really over. Sooner or later, he would have to come back, for one reason or another.

Salem Falls has always had its ghosts, and they are awakening at this very moment.

Mine, evidently, has just returned.

CHAPTER 3

Markus

Perhaps I shouldn't have, but I couldn't resist. While the shop was still open, I tried to sneak a peek without him noticing me. I hid in a corner and watched as the last customers left "Moonlight", and he gradually turned off the lights before closing up and retreating. He apparently lives upstairs. I saw the lights come on only a few minutes later. Feeling safe, I approached the place for a better look.

When I decided to leave, I immediately went back to my hotel. I tried every way to distract myself and avoid thinking about it. I watched a TV series, tried reading a book, and checked my social media, which I try to update regularly. I haven't posted anything yet, not even a single photo of Salem Falls. I don't even know if I want to tell the world I'm here, since Nevil and the publicist are already managing that for me. I usually like to share everything with my fans; that's why they follow me, love me, and recognise me more than many other writers whose faces are often unknown.

I, on the other hand, am a public figure. Perhaps also because, as my publisher, my publicist, and the agents who have followed one another throughout my career have often reminded me, people find me quite pleasant to look at. This also increases my earnings. And above all, theirs.

Despite my efforts to get the sleep I needed, I scarcely slept, mostly tossing and turning. I only managed to doze off towards morning, and I woke up feeling as if I hadn't rested at all. My mind continued to process images and sensations throughout the night, like a projector replaying the same picture repeatedly.

His face and his blue eyes.

His body.

Caleb Monroe.

His name always pressed against my chest whenever I thought of him, as if I was afraid to say it aloud, to make it real.

But now it really is real. And I wanted it, I mean, I asked for it. I could have avoided this place, as I have always done in recent years.

I have no idea how he'll react when he sees me. I don't even know if he'll want to talk to me or have anything to do with me, even if one of the events involving me happens at his shop.

Clearly, I can't avoid going to "Moonlight". My presentation is scheduled there for tomorrow night, and as much as I'd love to find any excuse, skipping it would be absurd. The festival organisers certainly couldn't have imagined my past relationship with the venue's owner.

And I, to be honest, am weary of running away. Even of avoiding this place, as if I can't make peace with myself or truly move forward.

Maybe that's why I accepted my publisher's offer. Deep down, I knew what I'd face in Salem Falls, including the risk of bumping into Caleb.

I'm preparing to go out. I pay closer attention to my appearance than usual, checking my face in the mirror. My dark hair is slightly dishevelled, my beard is barely visible, and my eyes are, unfortunately, a bit tired. Similar to when I sleep little or poorly, or stay up all night writing and thinking.

I still have the appearance of a man trying to seem calm and determined, but inside he's always in turmoil. I feel a storm brewing inside me.

Inevitably, I begin to wonder what he'll think of me when he sees me. Will he still like me? He might have checked my social media or followed my career. Although, knowing him, I doubt it. Well, knowing him, he probably avoided me like the plague!

Time has changed me, and I am aware that I am no longer the boy I was ten years ago. A few wrinkles around my eyes, a darker gaze. While the most "extreme" change has been internal, invisible to the outside world, I know that beneath this surface, the real Markus Leigh still exists — the same one Caleb truly knew, the one who loved staying up late talking about unrealised dreams and secret fears until dawn. The one who chose to write and act, rather than truly live.

Yet, I have a feeling he won't see it again. Perhaps because he'll refuse to see it. He won't see me.

I leave my room, head downstairs, and pass by the reception desk. Allie and another girl, a colleague I believe, smile and greet me with an ecstatic expression I've become accustomed to. A mechanism kicks in within me, too, prompting me to respond to the flirtatious smiles, compliments, and flattery. So I revert to being the same Markus Leigh I recently was. The famous one. The one who knows he's liked by more or less everyone.

But he won't like me. The immediate truth that flashes in my mind hits me like a thorn in the heart. He won't like me any longer.

Outside, in the morning glow, the town looks more lively and vibrant than ever. Shop windows sparkle with orange decorations, and the streets are filled with the aroma of caramel apples and hot chocolate. Passersby wear themed scarves and hats, with some even donning masks.

This is Halloween in America, sweet and spooky at the same time. And Salem Falls is, more than ever during this season, the epitome of Halloween.

I walk quickly, keeping my gaze lowered, hoping that the people I pass, lost in their own pursuits and pastimes, won't recognise me. Meanwhile, I try to keep my nerves in check. Every step closer to "Moonlight" feels like a return to what I had tried to banish from my soul, but which I have missed more than I can say.

This time, it will be different, I know. Because this time, I will no longer be able to just observe, hiding in the darkness.

Caleb's shop is located on the corner of a cobbled street. The dark wooden door features the sign I saw last night, which now seems even more captivating and evocative: "Moonlight Café & Bookshop". Perhaps it's because the window display, now illuminated by daylight, looks warmer, filled with carefully arranged books, Halloween-themed ceramic mugs, painted pumpkins, and white lanterns.

I try to calm down and compose myself, taking a deep sigh. Actually, two. Then I gather my courage and go inside.

The bell above the door rings sharply, almost theatrically. I look around. Inside, the place smells of vanilla, cookies, and coffee. I pause for a moment, letting my eyes adjust to the evocative golden dimness that dominates some areas of the bookshop. There are shelves full of volumes, velvet armchairs, and small round tables. The background music is jazz, soft, almost intimate.

This place is delicious. Truly, just what I expected.

I sigh and keep looking around, eager to notice every corner and detail, as if I want to absorb it all inside me so I can describe it once I've gone.

And then I see him.

Caleb is behind the counter, serving a customer. Now that I see him more clearly and up close, I realise that time has been far kinder to him. In fact, to be honest, it has even improved him from how I remembered him.

His hair is just a little shorter, slicked back, with a few dark blond strands partially falling over his face and catching the light. He wears a light blue shirt, with the sleeves rolled up slightly, revealing part of a tattoo, apparently tribal, that he didn't have ten years ago.

He's more mature, more of a man. But it's only when the customer says goodbye and steps away from the counter that I enter his field of vision, and his gaze settles on me. In his blue eyes, like a stormy sky, there's something I can't quite read immediately: surprise, anxiety, or perhaps even suppressed anger.

I know he was expecting me. Maybe not immediately, but he's certainly heard about the event I'm holding at his coffee shop. He might not have organised it himself, but if he agreed to host my book launch, he must have been supportive. Or at least I hope so.

At this moment, time truly stands still.

I stand here, still, unable to move closer to him. His gaze on me remains unchanged. Ten long years are contained within a single look.

'Markus.'

He unexpectedly is the first to recover and react, saying my name.

So, now it's my turn. I have to say something, anything, but my voice won't come out; it's caught in my throat.

'Hi, Caleb.'

I force myself to smile, but around him I feel awkward and inadequate, which is something I rarely do.

Caleb rearranges a few books, trying to create some distance between us and appear at ease. But I quickly notice that he's also struggling.

'I didn't think I'd see you here again.' He looks back at me and shrugs. 'In fact, I didn't think I'd see you again, ever.'

'Me neither, to be honest.'

He merely nods, without responding.

Thus, silence falls once more between us.

Also, because every word appears pointless to me.

I despise this embarrassment. I could try to explain, to say that I agreed to participate in the festival events, but I didn't know the presentation was being held at his venue. I could attempt to justify myself, to clarify my actions, but I know it won't help. Our eyes already reveal enough: ten years gone without a proper explanation, ten years of unspoken words, ten years of regret, at least on my side.

Then, of course, I moved on in one way or another. Also because, in the meantime, resisting and moving forward became my job. My mission.

'I would like…'

I try to say something, but a cheerful voice interrupts our awkward silence and eases the tension that has built up.

'Hey, Caleb. Any news from the festival organisers? Any word on the writer? I asked Steve, but he hasn't had any updates today either. He just knows he should be here by now!' She pauses briefly and chuckles amusedly. 'I texted your Aunt Leanne; she didn't know anything yet. You'll hear from her; you didn't even tell her her idol is coming to "Moonlight"!'

'Um... Chelsea...' Caleb clears his throat and nods towards the girl, looking at me. 'Her "idol" is here.'

'What?'

The girl, Chelsea, apparently turns towards me. She's young, lively, with long black hair and large green eyes. She's perplexed for a moment but quickly recovers.

'Oh my God!' She immediately moves towards me and enthusiastically extends her hand. 'Nice to meet you, I'm Chelsea Davenport. I help organise Halloween events. I mean, I try to help, but we're always late with updates when something changes! Anyway, I'm really happy to have you here, Mr Leigh.'

'Nice to meet you, Chelsea. You can call me Markus, if you like.'

'Okay, Markus.'

She smiles and tilts her head slightly before glancing swiftly at Caleb. Her eyes narrow just a little, as if she's sensed something, but I can't quite figure out what. She doesn't seem to know about us, especially since we've kept our relationship private. And surely, ten years ago, Chelsea would have been a teenager.

'The presentation's tomorrow night, isn't it?' I ask, just to fill the silence. Even though I already know the answer.

'Exactly, tomorrow night at six,' Chelsea confirms. 'We'll receive copies of your book this evening. The festival organisers will take care of everything else, including the signing and refreshments.'

'Good. Thanks, Chelsea.' I have to try to compose myself, to act as casual as usual. It's not Chelsea, it's Caleb who's stopping me. The way he's scrutinising me, as if he's examining my intentions. 'Can I... sit down for a drink?'

I turn straight to Caleb, gesturing at one of the empty tables. I need to hear his voice again.

'Yes, of course.' He nods with an almost unnoticeable movement of his head.

'Well, I'll have a ginseng coffee.'

'Sure, he'll be there in a moment.'

'Thank you.'

I go and sit by a window that overlooks the view.

I can't believe I'm here. I still find it hard to grasp being in his shop, with him just a few steps away from me. Caleb is working behind the counter, but I can feel him moving, breathing, as if each of his gestures were linked to mine.

When he approaches my table to serve me coffee, we are even closer. And I can sense his essence, his enveloping scent. The memory of his lips on mine, of his taste, is only a result of his proximity, but I feel my breath catch. As if my world, the one I've patiently built over these years, is about to burst apart. Or collapse.

I pick up the cup Caleb has placed on the table, but it almost trembles in my hands. I am sure he's noticed, yet he acts nonchalant.

'If you need anything else, just ask.' His voice is calm, but his eyes reveal his turmoil. My presence here definitely matters to him.

'Thank you.'

I say nothing more, and he walks away. I try to tell myself he's just doing his job, which is why he's kind to me. I sip slowly, while the taste of the coffee almost transports me back in time — to our conversations, our laughter. But now, it seems there's only silence, frustration, and anger between us. The words we exchange are merely courtesy and duty.

When I get up to leave, Chelsea has gone, and Caleb is stacking a pile of books on a shelf.

'I should pay for my coffee...' I step closer, looking for an excuse to speak to him again.

'Don't worry, it's on the house.'

'See you tomorrow, then,' I sigh, almost sounding disappointed. 'Thanks, Caleb.'

'Sure, see you tomorrow.' He turns around slightly and then continues his work undaunted. 'Thank you.'

I leave "Moonlight Café & Bookshop" with my heart pounding, feeling utterly in turmoil. I feel lost here, without him. Without truly having him.

And I understand, perhaps for the first time in many years, that no amount of time or distance can ever truly erase what remains unresolved between us.

CHAPTER 4

Caleb

I didn't think he would actually get into "Moonlight".

Not even when Chelsea announced his arrival for the presentation did I believe it. No, I still thought it was impossible, out of reach. I was so convinced he'd find some excuse at the last minute to avoid it.

But then... I heard the sound of that cursed orange pumpkin bell Chelsea had hanging above the door. I pretended not to notice his presence, continuing to serve the customer in front of me, delaying having to confront him for as long as possible.

I was almost certain I couldn't manage it.

And even now, to be honest, I still don't quite know how to tolerate his presence.

Ten years have gone by. Markus has changed; he seems more mature, both in his features and his gaze. His look is more captivating, and his manner is noticeably more confident and alluring. It appears he has trained, over the years, to be the centre of attention.

And yet, in some inexplicable way, he remains the same to me. He still bears the same absorbed gaze, the same cautious way of moving, as if his world might crumble and shatter at any moment. But now there's also a shadow in his dark eyes, something that makes him seem dull, perhaps even guilty.

The moment he said my name, everything I'd tried to suppress came rushing back. Now I can't quite identify what I feel. I know it's no longer hate. Not just hate, at least. It's like a dangerous mixture of surprise, resentment, nostalgia, and, as much as I hate to admit it, desire. Because the problem is, even after all this time, my body recognises him. My body still desires him. In fact, maybe even more than before. It's as if I've never forgotten his touch, his hands on me, his lips on mine.

When Chelsea returns to "Moonlight" after leaving under the pretext of a meeting with the festival organisers and to see her boyfriend, Steve, I have a strong feeling that my employee is carefully observing my every gesture, every look I make. As if she's sensed something on my part. Maybe it's just my impression; I feel transparent since I know he's here. It's not something that happens to me often, but it's certainly true that now, with Markus Leigh involved, I'm much more vulnerable.

'Not bad, our writer, huh?' Exactly. She looks at me suggestively. No, it can't just be my impression. Little Chelsea is too clever to be fooled.

'Yes, that's true.' I need to distract her; I don't want to talk about him. Not specifically, at least. 'Good, the participants will be delighted. That's the most important thing. Even for the upcoming writing workshops, I think.'

'Yes, that's for sure.' She nods and approaches, positioning herself on the other side of the counter and leaning on her elbows while resting her face on her hands. 'But what about you? What do you think?'

'What am I supposed to think?' Damn, the girl doesn't give up! 'You know he's not really my thing...'

'I know, but I mean... Markus Leigh lived around this area a bit, didn't he?'

Her green eyes narrow slightly at me. She's undoubtedly spoken to Aunt Leanne or someone else who's met him before. She's examining me with a detective-like expression, as if determined to make me confess my crimes at all costs.

'Yes, exactly. But...'

'Didn't you know him? I was too young, but you're about his age. Didn't you also arrive here in Salem Falls shortly before him, from Portland? I know Markus also took one of Julia's classes at "Callaghan Theatre".'

I huff and shrug. If only she knew how well I knew him!

'I didn't hang out with him much, actually.' I lie shamelessly. But I just can't bring myself to have this conversation with her. 'I mean, we didn't hang out in the same circles.'

And that's not even a lie; in fact, it was truly like that at first. I didn't go anywhere, except the theatre. Only because Aunt Leanne, being a friend of Julia Callaghan, had insisted.

'Ah, I see.' She now sounds convinced, despite her constant searching expression. 'I know he then left here and never returned. Perhaps he did the right thing; he found his fortune elsewhere.'

I nod without replying. I just want to change the subject now. To break up the conversation, I decide to better organise the desserts behind the display case under the counter.

Meanwhile, I reflect on Markus's gaze on me, even when I try to avoid or ignore it. I feel exposed, as if I am naked. It's as if he can still see right through me, as if I am back in my early twenties, when everything still seemed possible between us.

I've tried to be courteous and professional with him. After all, he's just another customer to me. The presentation of his book here at "Moonlight" will be similar to many others, like those of other authors, more or less famous, who have come before him.

But, inside, I was desperate to say something to him, anything apart from the usual polite phrases reserved for passing customers.

Something about us, as I found myself so close to him, I couldn't decide whether it hurt more to look at him or to pretend not to.

He's changed, undeniably, but his way of observing everything around him, including me, remains the same. And it devastates me, now more than ever. Even more so than when he chose to abandon me, walk away, ignoring me, my futile attempts to hold him back, to persuade him to stay.

As the morning goes on, I feel more lonely, even amid many people. Outside, the usual fog is lifting, almost intangible, but Salem Falls is so familiar with it.

I keep busy at the shop to take my mind off him. Even though I know it's only a temporary fix, since he's here and will probably stay for other festival events after the presentation of his new book.

I take a deep breath, feeling the usual mix of emotions rising inside me that I neither want nor can understand: anger, tenderness, fear, regret, and now a longing I fear I'll never be able to suppress. Especially now that he's back, and I'll be forced to watch him wander around, at least for the next few days.

But that's not the worst, in my opinion. Because it also brings the frightening and unavoidable realisation that, despite time and distance, a part of me has never stopped waiting for him.

CHAPTER 5

Markus

Ten years ago, Salem Falls evoked different feelings in me. Or perhaps I just had a different perception of life, myself, and what I aimed to achieve, sooner or later.

I was twenty-three, filled with ideas in my mind and too many insecurities to bring them to life. Many had put me down, telling me I'd never succeed. Among those "many" was my father. My mother obeyed him, even though she occasionally tried to accommodate me. Both, however, were more proud of my sister Eliza's professional and personal choices. With her degree in economics, she had always acted more prudently than I had, guided by logic and reason.

After leaving Providence, my hometown, and attending college in Boston, I unexpectedly found myself in Salem Falls because of a strange twist of fate. There, I took part in a summer programme in experimental theatre under the guidance of Julia Calloway, my college playwriting tutor. She was one of the few people who had shown even a flicker of faith in me and my talent as a writer and screenwriter. It was precisely in Salem Falls that I met Caleb and fell completely for him, with the intensity and impulsiveness of that summer. We were two lost souls who, together, rediscovered faith and hope.

Ever since I was a child, I had always been writing outlines for my future stories. At school, during lessons, at the park, while the other children dreamed of becoming football or baseball players. Even parties weren't particularly appealing to me. Around that time, I began to understand, without going too far, that I preferred boys to girls. After meeting Caleb, I was completely certain of it. Even if it wasn't exactly a preference, it was about him. It was always about him.

In any case, I was convinced that talent and hard work were enough to become a successful writer. I didn't realise that life would demand a higher price from me.

That summer, in Salem Falls, I felt overwhelmed by light and excitement. I believed I could create a world all my own. The sea reflected the sky like a mirror, and the days seemed endless. I felt free, as I had never felt before, to make my dreams come true.

I rented a studio apartment near the theatre and its attached theatre bookshop, "Calloway's Books", where I worked to pay for all the screenwriting and creative writing courses I faithfully continued attending, even remotely.

It was right there that I first met Caleb Monroe. I still remember the moment I saw him cross the threshold of the bookshop, his eyes shining with enthusiasm, his hair tousled, and the look of someone no longer afraid to face the world. Maybe because he'd already challenged it and lost enough. He was wearing a leather jacket over a white T-shirt and ripped jeans. As he approached me, he asked for my reading recommendations. Or perhaps it was simply an excuse to start a conversation.

'Do you have anything that keeps me awake at night?'

As he uttered those words, his eyes narrowed at me. I wondered if he'd realised the double meaning in his request. He appeared naive, but I was quite certain he knew he'd asked me an ambiguous question.

'We might try it. Maybe *White Nights*?'
'Yes, maybe.'

In any case, I smiled at him, and he smiled back. I felt a strange sensation, as if time had stopped and everything else in the world was about to fade away, leaving only us.

Caleb had a clear and perceptive way of seeing people. Yet, he could challenge others with merely a glance. He never looked away. I, on the other hand, was intimidated by everyone, barely managing to get by amidst hesitations and silences, constantly balancing between impulse and fear.

It was he who truly got close to me, who took the first step in trying to get to know me better. It was he who invited me for coffee, who persuaded me to go to the pier on the night of the solstice. And I let him, happy to surrender myself, day after day, to something I didn't yet understand, but that made me feel truly alive for the first time.

That was "the summer of my life", in a way, an extended pause filled with laughter, dreams, but most of all, confidences. It was as if we had emptied our souls to each other, even though the weight he bore on his heart was far heavier than mine. By writing our story, a story I would never publish, I had partly healed him. And I had also healed myself.

Perhaps I still didn't realise what would happen next, while those days and weeks were only a preview of the autumn that would change my destiny.

Caleb often told me that one day he would open his own café in Salem Falls, a place where people could read, enjoy a good drink, and simply feel at ease. A refuge for those in need. This was his dream: to help people feel good, or at least better. He hoped they would leave his café feeling lighter and more optimistic than when they entered.

Instead, I discussed with him the books I'd write and those I was already working on, as well as the characters who haunted me day and night, urging me to tell their stories. He laughed, teasing me about the constant stress my characters caused me. Nevertheless, he promised that one day he'd display all my books in his café-bookshop. In the meantime, using pseudonyms, I had begun publishing some of my stories online, entering competitions, and submitting the story I was most proud of to publishers.

'You can do it, I am sure of that.'

'I don't think so. I've chosen a path that's too hard. Maybe I should give up everything and find a "real job", as my father always told me. Perhaps I still have time to change.'

'No, Markus. This isn't what you really want.' He shook his head, placed his hand on mine, and looked me seriously in the eyes. He believed in me, too. 'Changing your path now is just the easiest way to make yourself unhappy. You don't have to do it. Promise me you'll hold on.'

'All right, Caleb. I'll try,' I sighed, shrugging. 'Maybe for a bit longer. If nothing changes, I'll realise that writing isn't my destiny, and I'll give up.'

Our bond gradually grew, day by day, amidst challenges to conquer and mutual support. When I realised this, I understood it would become increasingly hard for me to walk away from Salem Falls and especially from him. But I couldn't ignore what I truly wanted, what I had always wanted from the bottom of my heart: to succeed as a writer, to find myself in an environment that would further boost my career. If it meant using myself, my image, my charm, I would have done so without hesitation.

When the offer finally arrived from a prestigious New York publisher, it felt like a sign of destiny. However, it was really Julia Calloway, a longtime friend of the publishing house's founder's son, who opened the door for me and ensured they would consider my manuscript. It was my first genuine contract, offering the chance to present my novels to a wider audience who might enjoy them. But it also meant, sooner or later, leaving Salem Falls to better nurture my career's development.

I was still young, shy, and unknown. According to my new publisher, "Larsen Ink Publishing", people needed to see me and get to know me. I also needed to transform myself, becoming more confident, bold, and assertive. They strongly advised me to take part in literary events organised for me and other writers in my genre and beyond. They were investing in my image, not just my writing. They aimed to shape me as a "character", to build me as a celebrity to promote or sell to the world.

I hesitated before telling him. Then I realised that, unfortunately, I had no choice. I had to make a decision, and I couldn't miss the opportunity. I would regret it forever.

'You must go, if that's truly what you want.'

His voice was deep and almost distant, though his face seemed calm. After all, it was he who had encouraged me and convinced me not to give up. Even though he might not have imagined that I would be asked to live elsewhere and completely change my life and image.

I wasn't sure how to respond, not quite straightforwardly.

Did I truly want to go? Yes, the offer was too tempting to turn down. And, after all, it had always been my dream. I couldn't let it go, even if it meant... Yes, even if it meant losing him.

But I couldn't say it. Not truly, not while looking him in the face.

So, I didn't. I just left. I left a week after receiving the "Larsen Ink" proposal, towards the end of October, leaving a letter in the mail. Then I wrote to him again when I settled in New York. He didn't reply to my first letter, nor to the subsequent ones. He didn't even return my calls, emails, or texts. Essentially, he treated me as if I didn't exist. As if I'd never existed, to him. I kept pushing, for a little longer, until I realised I was carrying on a one-sided relationship. A love affair that, by now, only lived inside me and in the pages I'd written about us.

A few months after I decided not to write to or contact him any longer, I received a brief email from him.

"I hope you have found the place where you could write your stories, the life you desired. I'm still trying to forget you."

Hadn't he forgotten about me yet? Then why had he never replied to my letters, my messages?

I read and reread those few words countless times. This time, I was the one who didn't reply. Also, because I was certain he hadn't expected it anyway. That was his goodbye.

My first real book, *The Essence of Evil*, published by a major publisher who believed in me and my potential, was released about six months later. It performed much better than expected, and that marked the start of my success, which has now continued uninterrupted for ten years.

I could declare myself satisfied and happy. And I truly was! The thought of being liked thrilled me. Even my parents seemed proud of me. I had proven my worth. All those who had once doubted my talent were now seeking me out. But meanwhile, a void had formed inside me—a chasm had opened that no amount of recognition could ever fill.

Now, ten years on, I find myself back in Salem Falls, the town that truly shaped me, my awakening. I have actually sat at a table in the café-bookshop that Caleb only ever dreamed of so many years ago, but everything between us has changed. In fact, there is nothing left between us now.

Only by finding myself here again have I been able to grasp the extent of what I destroyed. And I wonder if, during that summer, amidst our confidences, kisses, and promises, we hadn't truly touched something eternal, something inviolable.

Maybe we did.

Maybe that's why it still hurts so much.

***

'I'll try to be on time for the presentation.'

Nevil's tone makes me somewhat suspicious, as if he doesn't fully trust me. I've known Nevil Larsen for ten years now, ever since his father, Clive Larsen, a friend of Julia's and son of the founder of "Larsen Ink", entrusted me to him as his personal challenge. Perhaps Clive didn't trust either of us very much, that's the truth. From my perspective, his main aim was to do Julia a favour. Instead, he tried everything with Nevil to involve him in the family business, even cutting off the funding for his costly vices and leaving him no choice but to finally get to work.

'Do you trust me that little, Nevil?'

'There, the question alone makes me doubt you. Markus, you know...'

Nevil is perhaps the only person in the world who knows the details of my story with Caleb Monroe. For one simple reason: he's read it. He's read everything I've ever written, in short—even the story I'll never publish.

'I won't mess things up, you know.' I huff and shift the phone from one hand to the other. 'If you doubt me so much, why did you encourage me to attend this event in Salem Falls?'

'Simple, it seemed like a good opportunity, given the time period and the theme of your book.'

'The theme's always the same in all my books, Nevil. Monsters, ghosts, more tricks than treats, spooky stuff. For ten years.'

'Mmm…' he hesitates and does not carry on.

Why is he hesitating? It's not in Nevil Larsen's nature to doubt. Not even at the beginning, when my career and success were still a big question mark. For him, I truly became a personal challenge.

'Is there anything else I should know?'

'All right!'

Now he sighs, annoyed. I imagine him narrowing his gaze at an indefinite point and adjusting his slim rectangular glasses. From a reckless boy, he's become a genuine intellectual in recent years. You could say he's settled down. His father was right, after all. Nevil has truly developed a passion for his work. And as his earnings and mine increased, I became more alluring and provocative, while he grew more serious and dull. His hair, which once hung past his shoulders, is now getting shorter and shorter, with not a single strand out of place. He practically resembles a carbon copy of his father and grandfather in their youth. Soon, his portrait will hang beside theirs in the large meeting room of the publishing house.

'All right, what, Nevil?'

Why the hell doesn't he decide to speak? What could be so serious?

'Your interviewer, Timothy Dawson, won't be there. He's got a bad flu and can't leave Boston right now.'

It's a pity! Dawson had written a glowing review of my book. And, as planned, he was travelling from Boston for the interview. It would mainly be a breeze with him. He loves my books and had interviewed me before.

'Have you found someone to replace him?'

'Yes, although he still needs to accept.'

'So? Who is it?'

I don't know what's wrong with him tonight. Nevil seems determined to drive me mad!

'He's a local, Markus.'

'Okay, that's good! At least we're sure he'll be there.' I sigh in relief. 'He can't escape from here!'

'No... let's hope not, that's all.'

'So, Nevil! Are we done playing guessing games? Who's this?'

'He's the owner of "Moonlight"… Caleb Monroe.'

CHAPTER 6

Caleb

I was twenty-two years old, and the whole world lay before me. Or so I hoped. Because after the destruction of my previous world, I was left with nothing else to hold on to. Hope was all I had left.

I worked as a bartender in a place that smelled of beer and fried food, but I had a thousand dreams. Even though I, at the time, often smelled of beer and fried food too.

To avoid becoming too reliant on Aunt Leanne, whom I had initially moved in with, I lived in a small apartment on the outskirts of Salem Falls. The area certainly wasn't the best, but I felt that, in a way, my real life was about to start. I still didn't know exactly where it would lead, but that didn't matter. I would adapt to whatever fate had in store for me.

Then, he entered my life.

Markus Leigh, driven by his determination and unstoppable dreams that many had already considered unattainable.

But he, even if he sometimes felt discouraged by the lack of immediate feedback, was determined to succeed, one way or another. From the beginning, this filled me with a mixture of fear and respect. I was afraid I wasn't like him, that I wasn't as committed to making my own mark in the world. And this led me to admire his boldness and resourcefulness. I envied him partly, even if I couldn't admit it at the time.

Markus's dream was to become a writer, whether novels or playwrights. This was also why he had turned to Julia Calloway that summer. He saw the theatre experience as a chance to get even closer to his "destiny", something that would help him grow as an author. He was certainly more motivated than I and others in this regard. For me, theatre had been more of a psychological lifeline. That's what Julia and Aunt Leanne called it. And all things considered, they were right.

Markus intrigued me from the very start, ever since my eyes first caught sight of him. It wasn't just the novelty of being the new guy in town; there was something more. He seemed to carry the aura of someone whose thoughts and imagination lived more vividly than the real world around him. That's why he immediately sparked my curiosity. There was a certain fragility about him, yet simultaneously, a depth I'd never encountered in anyone else.

From our first encounter in the theatre library, we started chatting. Then we began meeting more frequently. So much so that I became more diligent in attending theatre classes, just to be near him. I felt increasingly drawn to Markus, to the inner world he managed to create within himself, which, by being around him, had started to include me as well.

Markus was everything I wasn't: introverted, thoughtful, profound. I, on the other hand, was impulsive most of the time, acting on instinct and quickly burning out. I had a strong desire to laugh and enjoy myself, without much concern for my future, since the past had already caused me enough trouble. I had my dream — I hoped to open my own place someday — but it was nothing compared to Markus's burning aspiration to become a successful writer. I didn't share that drive, that spark that motivated him day after day.

Perhaps this is why, inexplicably, our relationship worked so well, even when we played the roles Julia entrusted to us together. We balanced each other, like two extremes holding each other in equilibrium. Our relationship wasn't calm, it wasn't peaceful. But it was real, at least from my perspective. And intense, as only loves born without defenses can be.

Markus kept jotting down notes in his notebook for the novels and screenplays he was frantically writing wherever he went: in his room, at the theatre, at work, or during our stop at some place along the harbour, watching the lights of Salem Falls twinkle in the evening.

He believed that all those notes would someday become stories. That his mind would shape them into incredible, frightening, and possibly even chilling tales. He was confident he had a natural talent for the genre, even if it was inspired by reality.

'Horror reveals people's true nature, without masks or filters. Don't you believe me?'

I chuckled, shaking my head.

'If you're so sure... I'd prefer something more reassuring. Like a happy ending, for instance.'

'Happy endings don't exist, Caleb. Not in real life.' He sighed and bit his lip, a hint of desolation in his eyes. 'Not forever. If you notice, even in books and movies, happy endings are always left hanging. We don't know what really happens next.'

'You're too complicated, Markus.'

So I tried every way to change the subject. In fact, I understood what he was saying perfectly well. But I didn't want to confront it, because it meant that our relationship was also "on hold", as if waiting for something that would shatter it forever.

I was proud of him, of his resourcefulness, of his ingenuity, and of his imagination—so fervent, so passionate.

When he received his first publication offer from a major publisher in New York, one of the most important to whom he had sent his manuscript, I noticed that the mixture of fear and desire in his eyes grew increasingly intense.

I knew how important it was to Markus, and I was proud of him, to see that all his hard work had paid off and that his talent had been recognised. He was so young and attractive that he would fully enjoy the rewards of the brilliant career that awaited him. But I also knew, at the same time, that he would never be quite the same again. I saw it immediately, from the look in his eyes. While he was still hesitating, I already realised he would leave, accepting the proposal he'd received with all its implications. Anyone would have done it, maybe even me. So much so that I would have preferred him to tell me the truth from the very first moment, instead of holding back, clinging to the new world we had created together over that summer in Salem Falls.

The truth... well, the truth is that I secretly suspected and therefore worried that Markus Leigh would only be a temporary part of my life. That he would have other relationships, build different worlds, and drift away from me. With others, perhaps he would meet someone better than me, someone who could help him grow without being confined to a narrow way of thinking, in a charming town that offered few opportunities. Just as I had desperately needed to shut myself away in Salem Falls, seeking safety, he needed to open himself up to the rest of the world, seeking recognition.

That's why I encouraged him as much as I could, even though, in my heart, I felt a crack widening and expanding until it occupied an ever-larger space inside my chest.

'This is a once-in-a-lifetime opportunity, Markus.' It was hard for me to let him go. But I realised it was the best choice for his career. I couldn't keep him; I couldn't be so selfish. 'I think you shouldn't give up; it might not happen again.'

'I know, but...' Watching him struggle with doubt hurt, even though I wished he'd stay. 'Maybe it's too soon; I risk getting burned. I'm afraid I'm not quite ready and that... well, that they'll take advantage of me, that's all.'

Taking advantage of him... The fact that he was young, attractive, and brilliant. Yes, perhaps he was partly right. But deep down, I knew it was an excuse, a ploy to try not to be too brutal towards me, claiming that his choice wouldn't include me, our relationship.

Despite his attempts to delay, I realised that a contract with "Larsen Ink Publishing" was what he had always wished for. His dream was becoming reality; he just needed to accept his fate and let it lead him to stardom and success.

Why was he hesitating?

For me? For our relationship? For the bond he was establishing with a place that had only recently become his?

I had no regrets, though. Thanks to him, I'd discovered who I truly was. And I couldn't forget that.

I would have accepted everything from him. Everything, truly, if only he'd been honest with me. Even if it was that he maybe didn't love me enough. I would have understood; I would have let him go.

Everything, but not a lie perpetuated day after day. Not the pretense of having chosen to give up something so important, only to then run away from me without a word, without a proper goodbye. As if he had left me hanging, waiting for a return that would never happen.

Only a letter of apology awaited me. Then a few more, written directly from New York, along with a few emails and messages.

It was the last week of October. The town of Salem Falls was growing busier with excitement for Halloween. The most popular time for everyone here, the most fortunate, the most thrilling. Even better than Christmas, if that's possible!

But not for me, not anymore. I had hoped to share it with Markus, who instead had gone, leaving a few written words in my mailbox.

I realised that he had no problem with writing, more than ever that day. He struggled with words spoken face-to-face and with the truth. He also seemed to have difficulty with genuine emotions, since he preferred fake ones.

So I hadn't realised that the last kiss we shared would really be our final one. That the final moment between us would never happen again, that I would never be able to touch his body, hold him close, snuggle up to him at night, have him in my arms, or let go without the oppressive feeling I had always experienced before him when it came to truly expressing who I was and what I wanted for myself.

'I'm not leaving you, I'm just trying to figure out who I am and what I want.'

This was the conclusion of his letter, at the end of words that meant everything and nothing to our relationship.

He wasn't leaving me, but he was walking away without actually confronting me?

He wasn't leaving me, yet he lacked the courage to tell me the truth, even when I had pressed him to consider his choices and future.

I read those words over and over again, until I nearly wore out the paper they were written on. So frequently that, eventually, they lost all meaning for me.

I avoided replying to him, except for a brief email months later, when I realised that by now I must have become just a vague memory to him.

"I hope you have found the place where you could write your stories, the life you desired. I'm still trying to forget you."

Gradually, I stopped waiting. Or at least I tried to. However, he didn't reply to my few words.

Then I realised it was time to start focusing on myself. To pursue my dream, even if it still seemed vague and unfocused compared to his. I worked even harder, tirelessly, to save the necessary capital. Aunt Leanne, recognising my motivation, decided to help me accelerate the opening of my "Moonlight Café & Bookshop", which, three years later, finally saw the light of day.

So more years went by. I remained here, with my shop and a few trivial relationships. Meanwhile, he became a renowned, established writer, respected and recognised by everyone, even in Salem Falls.

With "Moonlight", I have managed to rebuild my life and my identity, which I felt was lost when I arrived from Portland. But there are nights, especially in October, when the rain drums against the windows and the lights of Salem Falls flicker in the darkness, and I still seem to hear his laughter, feel the warmth of his hands on me, taste his kisses, and remember that summer now lost in memories.

And every time I wonder whether he, too, has retained some memory, some fragment of us. Or if it was only I, trying to rebuild myself and move on, who continued to live amidst the shadows of the past.

Shadows that, I now genuinely realise, have stayed silent, waiting for the perfect moment to resurface.

And now that Markus Leigh has returned to Salem Falls, I know those shadows have finally found their way. They're still here, all around me.

**

The ringing of the phone distracts me from my thoughts and the constant rehashing of the past that has haunted me ever since I saw him again. Perhaps it's for the best. Walking down memory lane is never truly pleasant for me, especially when it's about something I've lost and will never regain.

When Chelsea's name appears on the screen, I smile. I wonder what she has planned this time! She often comes up with new ideas to enliven the atmosphere at "Moonlight", she says.

'I have some good news and some... I don't know... maybe not so good, that's it!'

Oh my goodness, there she goes again. She loves playing these games.

'Okay, go with the not-so-good one.'

'Hmm...' she sighs and hesitates, and I don't understand why. 'The problem is, the not-so-good one is closely related to the good one, so... it gets a little complicated...'

'Okay, Chelsea. So the only option I have now... the good one first!'

'Here... "Larsen Ink Publishing" would be interested in organising additional events and presentations in Salem Falls, especially at your venue. The publisher really liked the idea and concept of "Moonlight". They haven't yet made a formal request to the owner — essentially to you — but they plan to soon. It's a bit of gossip I heard from Steve, one of the festival organisers, and... well, we've been seeing each other more often these days.'

'Well... that's fantastic!' I don't know what else to say, it sounds like good news. But she could have enjoyed the evening and told me tomorrow morning.

"Larsen Ink" is Markus's publishing house. Of course, that doesn't mean we should only showcase his books. Many other authors are represented by the imprint.

'I'm glad you like the idea, because now I'm afraid the news isn't so good.' Chelsea clears her throat; I hear her hesitate. 'And that's also why I'm calling you now. Because... Well, Timothy Dawson, the host and moderator of tomorrow's event, the one with Markus Leigh, unfortunately has come down with a bad flu and won't be able to be here.'

'Oh, I'm sorry...' The news, as far as I'm concerned, isn't as bad as Chelsea believes. Sure, I feel sorry for the host who was supposed to interview Markus, but... it's better this way, after all. At least for me. 'Does this mean the event won't take place?'

'No, not quite.'

'So?'

'That means there will be another interviewer, Caleb.'

'Well… no problem, one is as good as the other, isn't it?'

I don't understand why she's so worried about something that the festival organisers, Markus, and the publishing house are supposed to be sorting out. What have I got to do with it?

'Not exactly.'

'Chelsea… can you get to the point, please?'

'The point is… the other suggested interviewer is you, Caleb. "Larsen Ink" wants you.'

'What?'

Are they mad? Yes, they must be! I… no, I'm not the right person! I…

'I haven't even read the book, Chelsea!'

I haven't read any published books by Markus Leigh, but I don't think I need to point that out now.

'I know, but you can download it as an ebook. That's why I called you. If you prefer the paperback, I can bring you a copy.'

No, no! It can't be! It's unbelievable.

'And when should I read it? Tonight?'

'Yes, if you're able. It's about three hundred pages...'

'Let's say almost four hundred!'

'So, you've read up on it!' She chuckles now. What could be so funny? 'Anyway, if you don't manage to do it, I'll also forward you a summary and the questions that Markus agreed upon. But I assure you, the novel is very engaging, easy to read, and...'

'Why me?'

I'm the least suitable person. Anyone would be better than me at this point—another festival organiser like Steve, Chelsea, or even my aunt Leanne. In fact, my aunt Leanne would be ideal! She knows the complete works of the great Markus Leigh almost by heart.

'Markus asked for it, in agreement with his publisher. They want you, no one else.'

CHAPTER 7

Markus

The late afternoon light filters through the windows of the "Moonlight Café & Bookshop", casting the space in shades of orange, gold, and bronze — the typical autumn colours, so vivid and evocative, at least to me. I sigh quietly, sipping my ginseng coffee slowly. I hope it helps me focus and relieves stress.

Outside, Salem Falls is a scene of witches' hats, pumpkins, laughter, and the smell of roasting chestnuts. Inside, however, there's a strange silence all around me. The kind that threatens to come before a storm.

I haven't seen Caleb yet, and it feels really strange that he's not at his place. Perhaps we shouldn't have involved him personally. Maybe we made a mistake. He must have felt pressured, and that wasn't my intention. At this stage, it might have been better to postpone the presentation or cancel it.

Furthermore, a poster of the presentation featuring my face has been placed on the front window, and flyers are scattered around "Moonlight". This is quite typical in normal circumstances. However, I doubt it is, considering that the owner of the place despises me.

Nevil places the microphone on my jacket with the usual precision of someone who likes to be in full control. This isn't my first presentation; in fact, this one is quite modest compared to others at more prestigious events. I've also been interviewed on television several times. But in all the presentations I've given over the past ten years, I haven't interacted with Caleb.

'You're not nervous, are you?'

Nevil stands before me, watching me doubtfully and raising an eyebrow. He appears tense, the kind of expression he has when he thinks I'm about to mess up and then blame it on my "artistic temperament". He sighs and adjusts his glasses.

'Me? Are you joking?'

I grin cheekily, as usual. The trouble is, Nevil knows me too well to believe me. I don't know how he manages it, but he can usually spot the bullshit I'm spouting from miles away. Like when I assure him I've nearly finished the first draft of a novel, when in fact I've only written the first few chapters.

'You have the same expression as when I asked you to write the sequel to your first novel, *The Essence of Evil*.' He sighs again more deeply and folds his arms across his chest. 'And you know what came of it! A bestseller, an even greater success than the first. And that almost never happens with sequels.'

'Sure, a bestseller for you and a nervous breakdown for me. Thanks so much, Nevil.' I laugh it off; I have to hide the tension, and I have no choice at the moment. 'I ended up being so stressed that I slept for two weeks straight. And I would have carried on for another month, if possible!'

Nevil laughs and rolls his eyes. Anyway, when it comes to my emotional state, he's right. The feeling is generally the same. However, I doubt the outcome in this case will be as positive.

In any case, despite my efforts to lighten the mood, Nevil doesn't take the bait. He looks at me, his face now almost too serious.

'Do you want to tell me what's really going on?'

I shrug and try to avoid his gaze.

'You know…'

Of course he does. Nevil knows about me and Caleb. He is aware of my sexual orientation, even though we agreed not to make any formal statements about it and to keep the speculation going. Ultimately, the more people wonder about me, the more attention is drawn to my "image" of being out of reach that has been stitched onto me.

Maybe he thought I had moved on, and it was his idea to come here. Like seizing the opportunity and choosing Caleb as the official host's replacement. Of course, he couldn't have imagined the tearoom would be out of use and that Timothy Dawson would fall ill.

What is he thinking? What does he want from me? I can't figure it out. But in doing so, he's only risking exposing me, and that was never our plan.

'Markus...'

'The thing is, I haven't seen him in ten years, and now... it's as if not a single day has passed.' I can't help it, even though perhaps I should. It's all pointless now. Even subjecting myself and Caleb to this "torture" is pointless. 'Anyway, Nevil... let's finish this and then go back to New York, alright?'

'Markus, you can't go back. A lot has happened in ten years, and you know that too. You've grown, you've changed. We've all changed!' Nevil sighs, placing a reassuring hand on my shoulder. 'But... there's something you can do. And since you're a talented writer, you'll be very good at it. You can rewrite this past, use it.'

'Use it?'

'Exactly, use it. All this tension, this anger... this flame of passion burning inside you. Put it in your next novel, or... better yet, use it to revisit the one you had me read years ago. I think the time is right for that story.'

'Nevil, that novel, that story... Maybe I was a fool to write it. But I really should never have suggested it to you. We agreed to put it aside forever, to put it in a drawer and forget about its existence. It's the best thing for everyone.' I try to compose myself, grin, and roll my eyes. I don't want to think about it. And, above all, I don't want him to think about it. 'That's why you suggested I write the sequel to *The Essence of Evil*. And you were right! It's always best not to confuse readers with different genres, haven't you always said that?'

'Yes, of course. But...'

'But what?'

'But now, these novels—so intimate, introspective, and revealing—are enjoying great success. We could follow the trend and capitalise on the situation. Sparking it would be an excellent marketing strategy and also an opportunity for you to...'

'To come out?' I challenge him with a glance. 'Is that what you mean?'

Nevil always advised me not to do it, to keep it vague, lest I risk losing my influence with my audience. Now, apparently, he no longer seems so convinced. To be honest, public statements have never mattered to me.

'Yeah, well... it's your personal choice, Markus,' he says, glancing around as if eager to end the conversation, at least for now. 'But can you at least think about it?'

I nod, even though I'm not entirely sure I want to. In fact, to be honest, it still feels like a terrible idea. That story is gone, closed, forgotten... it wouldn't make sense to bring it up now. Besides, who would be interested? It's too intimate, too personal. It's so far beyond my standards that I've never managed to give it a title, not even a provisional one, as I've always done with all the others.

Perhaps it's because there's no way to name what happened between Caleb and me. To all the unspoken words that remained between us.

'Okay, I'll think about it.'

***

From my perspective, I can see that the private room at "Moonlight" prepared for the presentation is filling up very quickly. Meanwhile, I haven't even had a chance to meet Caleb or discuss the interview topics with him. This doesn't look promising!

Chelsea told me he was made to read my book all day and night. Nearly four hundred pages of my own writing! Far from "this flame of passion burning inside", he'll hate me to death now! Even more than before, if that's possible!

The moment of truth arrives. Most of the chairs are nearly all taken, with several people standing and others crowding the entrance to the room. After a brief introduction by Chelsea, Caleb enters, greeted by a short round of applause. He has a slight beard, blond hair slicked back, and blue eyes that seem to scan around him but never settle on any specific spot. He looks as if he'd like to be anywhere but here. Despite everything, he smiles and says thank you.

We only managed a brief glance at the back of the club, where Nevil was also present. I truly believe he did everything he could to avoid me. So, at this point, I don't know what to expect either.

Maybe he doesn't hate me, but I'm worried that forcing him to read my book wasn't a good idea. This presentation isn't a good idea either, damn it!

The evening is organised by the "Salem Falls Festival", in collaboration with "Larsen Ink

Publishing" as *"Meeting with the Author: Markus Leigh in Conversation with Caleb Monroe"*.

This alone doesn't look promising, to the point where I'm eager to run away, and I imagine Caleb is thinking the same thing right now.

What the hell was I thinking, agreeing to Nevil's proposal, coming back here? It feels like a nightmare, far worse than the ones I write about in my novels!

They changed everything at the last minute, including the meeting location and even the interviewer. So, they remade the posters and flyers for the umpteenth time. Sure, it can happen, but this really seems like persecution towards me.

Anyway, once he's greeted the audience, Caleb briefly mentions tonight's meeting. He's compelled to talk about me, my career, and my success as a writer. Meanwhile, I keep thinking everything is wrong, but it doesn't matter; we have to keep going.

Now it's my turn. I make my entrance smiling, and the applause is louder and warmer for me, but I feel nothing. In fact, I feel truly uncomfortable for the first time since the beginning of my career.

I sit on the stool beside him, facing our audience. We exchange a secret glance, and I get the impression that everyone here, absolutely everyone, can somehow read us, delve deep, uncover our past.

As if it were truly obvious, as if a mark had been stamped upon us. Next to him, I feel exposed, transparent.

Meanwhile, I feel the strength of his spicy scent; it hits me like a sweet punch in the stomach and rises to my head, almost causing dizziness. I wish I were elsewhere, with him. I wish...

'Mr. Leigh...' Caleb interrupts my improper thoughts. Our "conversation" begins, and I can't help but notice the ironic tone in his voice. 'It's a true honour to have you here in Salem Falls, in my humble "Moonlight".'

No, he's not just being ironic. He's sadistic, with his exaggerated detachment, and he's trying to put me on edge, I understand. Okay, he didn't say anything significant against me in those few words, but I know him well enough to pick up on the subtle cues.

'The honour is mine, Mr Monroe.' I can only follow him and maintain the same tone. 'I must congratulate you, you kept your promise.'

I turn towards him and notice his blue eyes widen slightly, as if caught off guard.

'Which one?'

'Opening this unique venue. I've seen few places that are so harmonious and so meticulously crafted.'

Now I truly want to see how he responds to me!

He doesn't reply straight away, just smiles. Perhaps he's considering how to fight back.

'Thank you. I certainly never imagined I would host such a renowned author and personally present his new book. A real surprise.'

Here, exactly.

The audience smiles and claps as we exchange compliments. They certainly don't notice the subtle tension that passes between us.

'Apparently, I'm quite good at surprises.' I can't help but retort.

Meanwhile, I notice Nevil, who's sitting in a chair at the front, staring at me. We should start talking about the book; that's what he's trying to say. Yes, I understand. Perhaps it's time.

'It's obviously a talent.' Caleb doesn't give up; at this point, it's not just up to me!

The audience, however, doesn't seem to mind much; quite the opposite... Everyone seems to enjoy our exchanges. But Caleb, at last, appears to have decided to steer the conversation towards the real topic of our "conversation". Not the two of us, but my book.

'Tell us about your latest book, Markus, *The Black Shadows of Vengeance*. What inspired it? Why did you focus so specifically on one of the most primal human instincts: revenge?'

No, perhaps not. Maybe he's not genuinely asking me about my book. He's talking about me, again. Or about himself. But, deep down, there's always a part of me in my books. That makes no difference.

'Precisely because it's one of the most primal human instincts. A bit like striving for power or...' No, I shouldn't have dashed in that direction! But I've done it now, and I won't stop. 'Or love.'

Caleb slightly narrows his eyes, seeming doubtful, but then nods.

'Yes, I agree.'

'The truth is that in books, movies, and even in our lives, there are only three fundamental elements around which all stories, despite their different variations, revolve: power, revenge, and love. These are what most often drive human behaviour.'

After this statement, the interview becomes more animated. Caleb follows me, and from his comments, it's clear he has actually read my book and knows it well. He's also careful not to give away too many spoilers, so as not to ruin the plot twists for those who haven't read it yet. I must admit, this surprises me, especially since I know he was forced to read it in such a short time.

We talk about my novel, the creative process that motivated me to write it, and how Salem Falls might have influenced me.

Then Caleb asks the question I've been waiting for all along.

'How much of its author is reflected in the protagonist? In that man who abandons everything to pursue an ideal of security and power, only to realise he has lost what truly mattered to him.'

'Quite a bit. Actually... a lot, I'd say.' I force myself to smile and seem relaxed, but inside I feel a lump in my throat tightening. 'But sometimes writing is the only way to express what you haven't had the courage to say in a long time. Writing is almost a cathartic experience, you know. At least, it is for me.'

He looks at me and remains silent. Then he briefly closes his eyes and nods.

'I understand.'

Just two words from him, while the audience around us erupts in thunderous applause. But I don't truly hear it; I only feel the rapid beating of my heart, as if all the past has come knocking once more. As if all the past has returned to me.

'Okay, thanks, Markus!' Caleb quickly takes over. I sense that, just like me, he's had enough of this meeting. He addresses the audience directly. 'If you have any questions for the author, we still have some time. Then we'll proceed to the signing.'

I give him a grateful look; the audience's questions are always the most enjoyable for me. This time is no different. Among others, Caleb's aunt, Leanne, proudly announces that she's started a book club in my honour.

'We meet once a month, to discuss your novels and the psychology of the characters.'

'I feel truly honoured, Leanne. I didn't expect this much!'

'You're our favourite author... after Stephen King!' she smiles amusedly, running her fingers through her blonde hair.

'But you're younger and more beautiful!' adds another lady of about the same age as Leanne, a supporter of the book club.

She is surrounded by a chorus of excited squeals.

'Thank you, ladies. But don't tell Stephen!'

Well, I'm the idol of the older ladies in Salem Falls. I glance at Caleb. At least someone here appreciates me! He smiles and shrugs. Maybe he wants to laugh in my face, but he can't.

Suddenly, a boy around ten years old raises his hand and waits for his turn.

'Will you stay for the kids' writing workshop?' He fixes his bright eyes on me, waiting for my response. Then, overcoming his embarrassment, he admits: 'I'd like to be like you someday... I want to be a writer!'

'I...' Damn! I was planning on throwing everything away and rushing back to New York after the interview. Not sticking around for another week or more. 'Um... sure I'll be there, right! What's your name?'

'Daniel...'

'I'm sure you can do it, Daniel. You'll be better than I am. I wasn't that motivated at your age.'

At the end of the meeting, as people queue for autographs, Nevil approaches with copies of my book and takes the opportunity to lean in towards me.

'Did you hear the audience? You caused sparks!'

'It doesn't seem like much to me... I mean, it was just like always. Except for the ladies' book club... that's noteworthy!'

I know where he's heading with this, so I try to play it down.

'You're mistaken, Markus. You should consider my idea.'

'I'd love to, Nevil. As always, anyway. The thing is, this time it doesn't seem like a good idea at all. To be honest, it seems like a shitty idea...'

'On the contrary! It's the best, I assure you. Take all this energy, revise, and finish the story. Consider the fact that it could become your turning point, your salvation.'

My turning point? My salvation? My way to overcome this pang of pain and loss that still afflicts me, suffocates me with bitterness and loneliness.

I look at him and realise that perhaps Nevil is right. So strongly that I could actually do it, I could truly approve of publishing that unfinished story.

But I don't want to think about it now. There are people queuing for autographs, and I want to focus only on them at this moment. And then, the truth is, a part of me fears that a new book, written and published, won't be enough to heal me. Not this time. Not permanently.

CHAPTER 8

Caleb

If someone had told me last week that I'd be interviewing Markus Leigh at my shop, I wouldn't have believed it. In fact, I'd have thought it was a trick. A nasty taste trick with no treat as a reward.

And yet, here we are. I tried right up to the very end to keep my distance, not wanting to be influenced by him and the feelings I still hold for him.

But when I saw him walk in, my heart refused to listen to reason. It still beats for him, and I can't persuade it that it's no longer right, that it's not worth it. Not for Markus Leigh.

Although he seems more mature and determined than he did ten years ago, today I realise that, deep down, his dark eyes remain the same. The way he looks at me, he lingers on me, as if he intends to investigate me, to discover me.

Markus Leigh's gaze, which could strip my body and heart bare without even touching me. His disarming smile, which drove me mad.

Neither of us held back in this challenge that was set upon me. I enjoyed teasing him, and he responded; the audience, meanwhile, enjoyed it alongside us, but secretly we played a game of innuendo whose rules only we knew, a language made of jokes, silences, and pauses that only we understood.

After the interview, we proceeded to questions from the audience. No one held back, not even my aunt Leanne, to the point that I started to fear they'd keep Markus entertained until late into the night.

Finally, Aunt Leanne herself, after having the nerve to get all the books in her possession signed and asking for a few photographs with him, approaches me smiling with the enthusiasm of a young girl who has just met her idol.

'Caleb, love! You were brilliant!' She cheerfully hugs me, her cheeks still flushed with excitement. 'How thrilling! This will be an unforgettable day for me and the girls in the club. It's a shame Julia isn't back yet... she'll be here in a few days anyway. She'll be so pleased to see you two together again... I mean... you were some of her top students!'

'Don't exaggerate, Aunt.' I smile and return the hug. 'We were... normal, that's all.'

She shakes her head, convinced. But I don't want her to force me to go back in time. Not now, and especially not here. I give her a pleading look, but I doubt it'll work. I've tried to avoid her words about seeing us "together again." I know Julia Calloway will return here soon. Although she now lives in Miami and travels the world frequently, she always comes back to Salem Falls around Halloween and remains for much of the autumn. For her, it's like a ritual to be here on October 31st.

In any case, Aunt Leanne doesn't give up. 'I think Markus misses this place more than...'

Fortunately, when she spots Chelsea coming towards us, she decides to hold back.

'You were fantastic!' Oh my, here's another! 'You have incredible chemistry! They did well to select you for the interview!'

Aunt Leanne nods enthusiastically. I wish I could vanish. But I can't, unfortunately.

'Chelsea, don't exaggerate. It was fun, I admit.'

'No, it wasn't just fun. It was... captivating, seductive... it was...'

'Okay, do you want to look up more synonyms?' I sigh and roll my eyes. I can't take it any longer!

'No, I give up!' she laughs and folds her arms. 'But tell me the truth, did you like it? His book, I mean. Did you really read it all?'

'Yes, Chelsea. I've actually read it all. Now you owe me a sleepless night!'

I won't admit I enjoyed it. I don't want to. I didn't even tell Markus during the interview; I managed to keep it vague. I don't even know if I enjoyed it, actually. I just know I couldn't put it down until I reached the last page. And not just because I was compelled to read it.

'I always told you he was a wonderful writer, a true talent.' Aunt Leanne gives me a sulky look. 'You never wanted to listen to me.'

I've never doubted Markus's talent. In fact, I've always believed in it and supported him. My issue with him and his writing is entirely different. But I definitely won't sit here and explain it to them.

'If you think you're going to convert me to your Markus Leigh book club, you're wrong, Auntie.' I laugh, gently stroking her back. 'It's not my genre. I only read this book because I had to, because of the interview.'

I glance over at Markus; he's still signing autographs and taking pictures with his readers. However, I notice the gaze of his publisher, Nevil Larsen, oddly fixed on me. I know he's the one who has guided Markus from the very start, when the publishing house decided to publish him on his father's recommendation, and has personally supported him throughout his career. So, in addition to being his publisher, he's also his friend and adviser. Markus owes much of his national and international success to him.

I imagine he'll want to speak with me about organising more events at my venue, as Chelsea had mentioned. I'm not sure if that's a good idea. It might mean Markus will return for further events and presentations. Honestly, I still don't know if I'll manage to get through today while he's still here sharing his success with Salem Falls. With me.

I still can't tear him from my heart, that's the bitter truth. I can't. His looks, his gestures, his kisses, are still imprinted within me. As are the words he spoke now, in an excerpt from our interview, hanging in the air like an echo of the time we shared together.

"…sometimes writing is the only way to express what you haven't had the courage to say in a long time."

Is that really the case? How much more of him, of us, might I discover in all his books I've refused to read? And in those he'll write in the coming years?

Perhaps a great deal, or perhaps nothing at all. I don't want to find out because it scares me.

Writing to express what you lacked the courage to say.

Does he truly believe that?

I fix my gaze on him, on my Markus, who has now become the acclaimed writer Markus Leigh. I shut out everything else, everyone else.

Maybe tomorrow I'll be able to speak to him again if he decides to stay. Or I'll try to avoid him, I'll let him go if he chooses not to stay any longer. The truth is, since that summer, I've never stopped thinking about him. In many different ways, I admit. But I've never truly been able to banish him from my heart. But now... now I'm tired, now I know I can't go on like this any longer.

I need closure. I need to break away from him once and for all. I need a life where Markus no longer has free rein. And that depends entirely on me, not on him. Because he made his choices, achieved his success, and fulfilled his dream. I've only tried, but it's almost as if I've been living off his reflection all these years. Partly, I hate to admit, waiting for his return.

It doesn't have to be like this anymore. I need to regain my freedom, my self-confidence. I can do it. I owe it to Salem Falls, to "Moonlight", to the people who visit my shop and have always trusted me. But, above all, I owe it to myself.

CHAPTER 9

Markus

I've decided to stay in Salem Falls for the rest of the festival. Also, because after my interview, I'll be attending other events as a guest and the scheduled writing workshops. I could have chosen differently; I wasn't forced to. I could have made up an excuse, a sudden, unavoidable commitment. But, in a sense, I had given my word, and the hotel is already booked. And besides, I can't disappoint a child who dreams of becoming a writer like me.

Although… no, it's all bullshit!

The truth is, I mostly decided to stay for him. And for that Halloween I never really experienced here in Salem Falls. But it was a Halloween I had dreamed of sharing with Caleb.

This isn't an attempt to reclaim the past from me. I'm not even sure I want to publish that story that Nevil, inexplicably, seems to care so much about.

It's about preserving the present, as far as I'm concerned. Perhaps even the future.

Another day here, and the streets seem to pulsate and buzz even more, with colours, laughter, masks, music, candles, pumpkins, and glowing lanterns. And in the midst of it all, I feel like a ghost who has returned to walk among creatures happy to live and share all this joy, all this enthusiasm.

The day after the presentation, after attending the inauguration of the workshops for children and adults held in the school gym, I allow myself a bit of freedom. I tried my best to be, as usual, productive and lively, to engage people in the various creative writing projects. But in reality, I feel exhausted and drained of energy.

The urge to return to "Moonlight" is strong, but I'm trying to resist. This isn't the right moment; I need a pause, to reflect, before I can clear things up with Caleb. I believe he needs it too, maybe even more than I do. I don't want to overwhelm him, nor do I want to impose my company any more than I have since I came back here.

Last night, after the presentation, when I had finally finished signing autographs and taking photos with the readers, I thanked Caleb, Chelsea, and the other organisers before leaving the venue with Nevil. For obvious reasons, I couldn't speak to

Caleb alone; I didn't even try. Nevil brought up the subject of the book I had written so many years ago, and I, mostly out of exhaustion, indulged him. He said he had already started editing the section I had sent him to read, aiming to speed up the process while waiting for me to return and finish it. He's convinced it's the right novel at the right time, and next year, around this time, it will really be a hit. To me, it's just a story that made sense when I wrote it, maybe even when I sent it to Nevil. Now... I don't know, it seems absurd to bring it back. It's the past I have let go of, that I have lost, and that can never be reclaimed—fragments of real life that I doubt anyone would care about. I want the present, now. And the more I think about it, the more I desire it with a strength I fear I can't control.

But the truth is, I'm not very eager to commit to a new project that Nevil will almost certainly soon ask me to undertake. I feel too exhausted, too confused, and too drained, so I might as well revisit an old one. My publisher hasn't even considered the possibility that this is entirely different from the genre my readers are accustomed to, even though it contains a substantial dose of drama, anguish, and mystery. He's confident it will succeed. He thinks it won't be a problem; my readers will keep following me and appreciate what I do. In fact, they'll be pleased to see me in a new light, more spontaneous and natural, where a few more emotions will come through.

I wander through Salem Falls, my thoughts racing, my throat tight, my mind flooded with memories I've never truly let go of. I keep walking without stopping, almost getting lost in the alleys of the town centre and venturing into more isolated and remote areas, seeking some space to breathe.

I need to find myself again. I crave silence and so much more that I don't even know how to ask for or express right now. I need him, to be honest — Caleb. A clarification, but not only that.

I sigh and carry on my way. Thankfully, no one recognises me. I've wrapped an orange Halloween scarf around my neck and wear the wizard hat the kids at the workshop gave me, which covers my head and most of my forehead. I'm trying to blend in. A writer rarely attracts the same public attention as an actor or singer. I don't always get recognised, but it happens quite often, especially after a presentation. Today, I'd really like to avoid that.

I look around. Moving further away from the town centre, amidst the festive atmosphere of events, music, and games of all kinds, I head towards one of the most significant sites from my previous visit to Salem Falls. Even the lights are dimmer in this area. The Halloween lanterns don't shine as brightly, and the setting seems softer, more subtle.

I sigh, remove my wizard's hat, twirl it in my hands, and keep walking. If I had any doubts before, now I am certain of my destination. There's not much further to go, I'm nearly there, and I have no plans to turn back.

I realise that it doesn't make much sense, except as a true dive into the past that would only serve to emphasise the melancholy that oppresses me after my arrival in Salem Falls, after seeing Caleb again, after the presentation of my book at his place.

Although, in truth, it's a lingering melancholy that has persisted with me for ten long years. Ever since I left him a letter and walked away, because I could never have done it while looking him in the face. No, looking him in the face, I could never have abandoned him. I might have lost my dream forever, but not him.

I stop suddenly, trying to get my bearings. The area is genuinely dark, darker than I remembered. But perhaps that's obvious, considering that the "Calloway Theatre" has been closed for quite some time now. About seven years, if I'm not mistaken. Ever since Julia Calloway decided to retire permanently and end her career with one last show she'd invited me to perform in. I would have done so, had it not been for the promotional tour for my new book, which "Larsen Ink Publishing" had already organised for me. Or perhaps the tour was just an excuse I found to avoid dwelling on the past, to avoid facing what I'd left behind.

'Your success pleases me too, but sooner or later you'll come back, dear.' Those were Julia's words, spoken over the phone in her cheerful, melodic voice. Now that I'm here, they echo again in my mind. 'And when that happens, you'll do it to stay, to continue your true story.'

I sigh and take a few more steps, regaining awareness of my surroundings. Despite the moment of confusion, I know exactly where I am and where I want to go. Meanwhile, however, a few drops of rain have begun to fall. I raise my eyes slightly to the sky, which has suddenly become threatening, and put on my wizard's hat again.

I immediately realise that it will do me little good, as the rain is gradually intensifying from a few drops into a torrent. I lift my head again when a flash of lightning splits the sky, followed by a clap of thunder.

The residential area here is more restricted, and I'm convinced that a good portion of the population has flocked to the centre. I bite my lip; the only sensible option seems to be to carry on to my destination, even though I don't think I'll be able to find shelter inside. If I headed back towards downtown Salem Falls, I'd still get soaked. Perhaps I should have taken the car.

I walk quickly, then suddenly stop. Maybe I'm losing it, but I have a clear sense of hearing footsteps behind me. Perhaps it's just someone trying to scare me for fun; after all, it's the right moment. I don't think it's dangerous. Or at least I hope not. Still, my heartbeat inevitably quickens. I start walking again, then halt once more and turn sharply, looking around.

'Markus...'

I recognise his voice before I can see him in the darkness, which now seems even thicker than before. So much so that I can no longer distinguish the lights from downtown, or even those of some nearby houses.

'Caleb?'

'Yes, it's me.'

A few moments later, I see him standing before me. His blue eyes are as stormy as the sky above us, his hair now wet from the rain, and he has that slightly lost look I've always adored.

'You were...' Maybe I shouldn't say it, even though it seems quite obvious. I don't want him to take it personally. And above all, I don't want him to leave. So I'll leave the sentence unspoken.

'Yes, I was following you,' he admits candidly, without making excuses. 'I'm sorry.'

'No, I...' I swallow hard. It's raining even more heavily, but I don't care. Not about the rain, not about getting soaked to the skin, not even about the risk of falling ill at this point. 'I don't mind, though.'

'I saw you and noticed you were heading in this direction.'

I nod and offer a faint smile.

'I just wanted to see it again, before...'

Another flash of lightning tears across the sky, then the crash of thunder makes me jump, even though I was expecting it.

'Let's go!' Caleb gestures towards the road that leads straight to the "Calloway Theatre". 'I believe there's been a widespread power outage.'

Exactly. That's why the lights of the town centre and the houses nearest to the theatre suddenly vanish. I nod and follow him without hesitation.

And so, in the darkness, I feel as if I am truly travelling back in time. Indeed, it seems as though no time has passed between us. Those ten years have been nothing more than a figment of my imagination, a terrible story I wrote but left unfinished, like the one I sent to Nevil.

Caleb leads the way, and I follow. I don't want to think about anything else right now. In fact, I am tempted to take his hand and pull him closer. But I resist, fearing I might break everything. That shy flicker between us, while the rest of the town suddenly fell into darkness.

We arrive at the "Calloway Theatre" and I pause to admire the Victorian-style building, the commanding white brick and sandstone structure that has meant so much to me, with its slightly faded sign.

Caleb also stops and turns to face me.

'Markus… we can come in, if you want.'

'Really? I thought it was closed after Julia…'

Regardless, I smile and nod, not letting this opportunity slip away. We rush towards the main entrance. Only when we arrive do I realise Caleb has the keys.

'Julia has retired to Florida and has been travelling the world since her retirement from the stage,' he explains once we've opened the front door and stepped inside. 'But she always comes back here for Halloween. I believe her connection to Salem Falls is unbreakable. In any case, she left me the keys to the theatre; I stop by to check on it now and then.'

'Well, at this point... thank you for following me.'

'Don't thank me. Look at the headlines in the papers: 'Famous Author Missing in Storm' wouldn't have attracted many tourists here in Salem Falls!' He chuckles and wrinkles his nose in a seductive grimace that sends a wave of desire through me I can't suppress. 'I did it for the sake of it, that's all.'

'Oh, sure. I can understand.' I nod and run a hand through my wet hair. 'Interest in Salem Falls and the potential revenue the town might lose.'

'It seems obvious! If you didn't know, my place is right in Salem Falls.' Caleb lifts his face, now challenging me with his gaze. Then he looks away and points to the inside of the theatre, the stalls, the stage. 'I know there's nothing exceptional here that you haven't seen many times before, but... do you want to take a walk while we wait for the rain to stop? I think the lights will be back on soon.'

'Yes, that's what I'm here for, after all. Although I wasn't expecting to get a look inside.'

I'm trying to calm my instincts. Seeing him like this, just a few steps away from me, his clothes soaked and raindrops falling from his hair onto his face, threatens to make me lose control. I know it, and I think Caleb understands it too. But I'm not sure this is what he wants from me.

We walk silently in the dark, past the stalls and rows of red seats. I remember everything as if it happened yesterday. Now more than ever, I feel like a ghost tiptoeing through its own past. Accompanied by another ghost I desperately want to touch but will never be able to hold or grasp.

Caleb is right. There's nothing remarkable here now that it's been abandoned, without the lights, sets, actors, and audience that once brought this place to life. Without Julia Calloway, above all, the true soul of the theatre. The one who, in her own way, also gave life to our relationship. But, in a sense, it's "my place", one of the few that truly meant something to me — more than others I've frequented, whether regularly or not, over the past ten years.

We reach the stage in silence. Caleb briefly turns to me, then climbs the side steps, resolute in his ascent. I watch him with my gaze; his tall, slender figure stands out in the darkness. He approaches without once taking his eyes off me.

'As you can see, it hasn't changed much.'

It's true. It once had an old-fashioned charm too, but now it's tinged with the scent of wood, dust, and perhaps even a past yearning to breathe again. As if this theatre longed for its better days, demanding someone restore its soul through performances that, sadly, will no longer be staged there.

'No, he hasn't changed much...' I admit with a strangled sigh. 'It's just... it's just sad, that's all.'

'I know. As if it had been abandoned and...'

Caleb pauses, suddenly turns his back on me and walks towards one of the wings. Instinctively, I rush to the steps, which creak even more under my weight, climb onto the stage, and join him.

'Caleb!'

My heart beats faster, as if I have travelled such a distance that it leaves me breathless. He doesn't turn around; he walks past the stage. I follow him behind the curtain, reach out, and manage to seize his wrist to hold him back.

He turns and gazes at me. His eyes are now locked onto mine.

We are truly alone for the first time after years of separation and detachment.

No audience. No jokes. No defenses.

'This place...' he sighs, biting his lip. 'It always seemed to me that everything was possible here. That everything was achievable. As a child in Portland, my parents often took me to see magic shows. Back then, I deluded myself into thinking that everything was fine and that everything would be okay. Maybe that's why the theatre always gave me this impression, of a place where dreams could come true. For a while, I dreamt of becoming a great magician. Precisely to make all dreams come true, even the impossible ones.'

'Well, I think you managed it, somehow.'

I let him go and miss his skin pressing against mine.

A new, nearly unnatural silence falls between us, as if he no longer wishes to carry on talking to me or to respond.

'Ten years...' he whispers softly. 'It took you ten years to come back here, Markus. And only one summer to...'

He doesn't go on. He drops his face, shakes his head.

'I hurt you, Caleb. I know.' There's no point in trying to justify myself; I must accept responsibility. Face his contempt, if necessary. 'But the truth is, I hurt myself too, more than I ever thought possible.'

'You had your dream to fulfil.'

He responds immediately, without hesitation, as if his reply were a pre-prepared phrase meant for me that had been running through his mind for a long, long time.

'I had my dream here too. I shouldn't have lost it.'

I raise my hand, reaching out again to make contact with his body, but I am unsure whether this time he will be willing to accept me or turn me away.

I manage to touch his shoulder with my fingers, and he doesn't flinch. So I squeeze it with my hand, then caress it. I take another step closer to him.

'I got the one thing I never wanted.' I grasp it with my other hand, gazing into his eyes. 'Hurt you. I didn't care much about making you hate me, but I never wanted to hurt you.'

'Yes, you hurt me. But I've never truly been able to hate you.'

Our words hang in the air, like lines spoken in this abandoned theatre. Like rehearsals played out backstage. I feel the agitation surge through my heart and then spread across my body.

'Why?'

After my simple question, I find myself holding my breath.

'Because you were my world, Markus. You were my home, even when you were gone.'

He raises his hand and brushes his fingers across my face. He holds them there for a moment, then pulls away. I, however, try to hold him back, drawing him even closer to my body and my lips.

I run my hand through his damp hair, stroking the back of his neck. It was a gesture he always appreciated, one that made him feel good and relaxed when he was feeling tense.

I feel the warmth of his skin, then I notice him shivering more and more. I'd like to say a thousand things, but none of them seem right. Not in my mind, not in my heart.

So I can't help but act, using my body and senses. I decide to take a risk, as I've wanted to ever since I saw him again. I pull him close and kiss him on the lips. I feel him resist for a moment, then give in, opening his mouth and letting my tongue intertwine with his.

Meanwhile, our bodies seek one another, hips pressing close, desperately searching for a lost world, perhaps not yet uncovered, not entirely.

I quickly remove his jacket from his shoulders, running my fingers down his chest beneath his jumper as Caleb pulls me closer and kisses my face and lips more passionately, with a fervour that makes me vibrate like I haven't in ten long years.

'I want you…' I sigh against his lips as I push him against the wall and move my hands to his hips before focusing on the zip of his trousers.

'Markus…'

Caleb makes it easier for me by letting himself go completely, following my movements as I turn him and press my erection against him. He moans, letting his head fall back onto my shoulder, while I shrug off my jacket and sweatshirt to feel his skin against mine even more, his heartbeat matching mine.

It's us again. We're back to the place where one of our first moments, our first kisses, happened.

So we move in harmony, like a dance that needs no rehearsal.

These ten years hardly seem like they've passed. It feels as if we've been living through everything together constantly.

Moaning again, against his lips, I meet his eyes for a moment — the stormy sky that drove me mad so many years ago. The realisation is instant, at least for me. I'm in love with him.

Yes, I'm still in love with Caleb Monroe. And now I am certain that nothing, not even my ambition, not even ten years later, can erase the feelings I hold for him.

I'm back. Maybe not to stay, but I am back. And whatever happens, I have only one certainty: I will do everything I can to get him back. I will do everything I can to never lose him again.

Finally, just as Julia Calloway warned me it would happen: I'm back to continue my true story.

CHAPTER 10

Caleb

When I saw him walking towards the "Calloway Theatre", I followed. I didn't even question whether it was right or wrong; I just knew I couldn't resist. I felt like some kind of obsessed stalker, but I didn't care.

Instinct guided me. At a certain point, I wanted to reveal myself; I knew he would want to see the inside of the theatre, but I wasn't so sure he wanted me around.

Then the storm erupted, and all the town lights suddenly went out. It was as if someone had flipped a switch to stop the party in progress, and we too were left frozen in the dark, frozen in time.

Perhaps it was another sign from a universe that enjoys complicating my life. Or, at least for once, it decided to meet me halfway. Somehow, it forced me to face reality, to stop pretending.

Markus's gaze fixed on me was unreadable, his dark eyes seemed distorted, caught somewhere between fear and relief.

Ten years. Ten years, yet it only takes a moment for me to remember why I fell head over heels for him. Ten years, and I still desire his body like no other before or since. Ten years, and I still crave his lips, his breath mingling with mine, his pleasure igniting with mine as I run my hands over his hips and let myself be carried away by his touch, by his movements that seek me until they transport me to another realm, where only the two of us exist.

Without a past. Without judgment. Without even this present that threatens to hurt and separate us again.

There has always been something about Markus, something that remains and compels me to protect him, while also pushing me to make him reveal everything he is hiding, everything he has always kept concealed, perhaps because it is part of his nature as a writer, part of his creative instinct.

The "Calloway Theatre", still beautiful even in its abandonment, has reawakened our primal instinct to seek each other, to possess each other, and to let ourselves go completely beyond the misunderstandings and pain that have endured through all these years of separation.

Somehow, from the first lightning bolt in the sky that signalled the storm, we found ourselves complicit once more, just as we always had been before.

So, we relived our first kisses, the impulsive growth of our love. As if suddenly, time had twisted itself to give us a second chance. Or to torment us, driving us utterly mad.

I hold onto him, still pressed against the wall, feeling so weak and so shocked that I could slide to the floor, dragging him with me.

'Caleb…' he whispers my name, his hoarse voice sounding as if it might break.

I expect him to speak, to say more; instead, he remains silent. Only his dark eyes, like burning coals, seem to convey the words I, at this moment, genuinely long to hear. The simplest truth, and perhaps also the most challenging.

Anger, desire, regret… but above all, that love which has never faded for me, has never ended.

I've never managed to get over what I felt for Markus Leigh. And the truth is that in this silence, here and now, in our shared sighs, and as our hearts beat as one, we're already revealing everything to each other.

'It was impossible to forget you.'

These are the first real words he's spoken to me, after the kisses, after the sex, after this attachment that keeps us from parting. He says them almost hesitantly, though, as if afraid of breaking the spell that's been woven between us.

'Me too,' I admit, wholeheartedly.

Markus offers a slight smile, his eyes partly closed.

'I... I wrote about you in every story, even when I pretended it wasn't you.'

'Considering you write horror...' I smile, tilt my head slightly, and brush my lips against his neck. 'I don't know how comforting that is.'

He laughs and pulls me by my waist.

'You've never read any of my stuff, have you?'

There, he caught me. 'No, apart from the unfinished one, the draft you sent to your publisher. And the last one, of course, but in this case I was compelled.'

'Why, with all my drafts?' he continues laughing and runs a hand through my hair. 'I remember correctly, I forced you.'

'That's not true. In that case, I did want it. And besides, I didn't have to interview you in front of your many readers. And with my aunt and her book club, who claim to be your number one fans!'

'You're mistaken, Stephen comes first!'

'Sorry, he's the king… you're not!'

We laugh together, after I don't know how long. We stay still for a little longer and then, as if by mutual agreement, we try to compose ourselves and slide down until we're sitting with our backs against the wall.

I turn towards him, his head moving closer to mine, and our foreheads touch in a gesture that is part of us, part of our relationship.

Markus tilts his face, seeking my lips. We share a tender, almost innocent kiss. But it's still just another touch, enough to rekindle everything between us. An ancient, familiar warmth, rising slowly like a flame until it sets my heart and senses ablaze.

Meanwhile, however, I realise we can't stay hidden here forever. Markus seems to be lost in my own thoughts, and so, in a few moments, the magic fades. We look at each other and it's still us, but now completely immersed in the present.

I try to move, determined to get up. I know the longer I wait, the greater the risk of hurting myself, now that our desire has been consumed and our flame has exploded. I don't want to find my heart in ruins, not again.

'Caleb…' Markus, instead of copying me and rising, remains steadfast in his stance.

'Mmm…?'

I put on my jacket and glance at him almost absentmindedly, as if I didn't care. I wish I didn't have to respond to him or even listen to what he might say. But, above all, I don't want to see rejection or regret in his eyes.

'It doesn't end here, does it?'

His gaze upon me still seems passionate, but tinged with an anguish I cannot comprehend.

'What?'

Markus finally decides to get up, grabs me by the shoulders, and fixes his eyes on mine, stopping me from looking away.

'You did understand.'

He's waiting for my response, I know. This suggests he's uncertain about me, about my feelings for him. But the one who left, abandoning everything, was him, not me. He was the one who shattered our relationship.

'Yes, I understand.'

I respond to him, moving towards the stage, intending to cross the stalls and then reach the exit of the "Calloway Theatre".

I hear him sigh, and then he follows me, muttering something indistinct. I try not to laugh.

'You're going to drive me mad, aren't you?' He reaches out, grabs my arm, then slides his hand down to clasp mine. 'Trying to win you back...'

'Hmm... I'll drive you mad as much as you deserve, Markus Leigh! Besides, I remind you that I was forced to read your four-hundred-page book in less than a day. You owe me a sleepless night! Do you accept the challenge?'

'You'll have more sleepless nights, I assure you. Do you want to try me?' He holds me back, forces me to face him, and leans in to bring his lips to mine with a sigh. 'Anyway, yes, Caleb Monroe. I accept the challenge. Will you wait for me?'

'Okay. I'll wait for you.'

CHAPTER 11

Markus

I toss and turn in bed; perhaps too many emotions are preventing me from sleeping.

The truth is, I would have liked him here with me. However, Caleb believed it was best to proceed cautiously. At this point, rather than staying at my hotel, it would have been easier to slip into his apartment above "Moonlight" and then into his room.

Anyway, I'm willing to wait and give him time. I'm prepared to work hard to win him back. There are far too many people milling about Salem Falls at the moment. Caleb and I need some peace and quiet to reconnect and decide our future.

Our love has resurfaced, and I am certain of it. Even if neither of us has yet found the courage to admit it. Though still fragile, it's an undeniable spark that, within me, has already become a flame. Everything returns to me like an echo that never fades, and I am convinced that fate is set to give us something precious, something magical.

I held him in my arms once more, softly caressing his body. I kept him close, not just in a dream that left me with nothing but regret by morning. Caleb was truly mine again.

But now, daylight will reveal what darkness has exposed and rebuilt for us.

It's only six o'clock, but I decide to get up since I'll never be able to sleep again. I go to my bedroom window and see that Salem Falls is shrouded in a thick fog that discourages me from going out. But I definitely will, as soon as "Moonlight" opens. I want to see him, to be with him, in every way possible. Even if, for now, he might not let me touch him.

I grab my laptop and go back to bed, taking the chance to jot down some notes, some "free thoughts" that might eventually prove useful for a story.

I work for over an hour, absorbed and focused on developing a new plot, then I jump at the sound of a notification.

I smile, hoping it's him, but my enthusiasm wanes when I realise it's Nevil. What on earth does he want so early? We had agreed he'd leave me alone, at least for a few days, while I focused on the workshops I had committed to attend.

I open the message and see that he's forwarded me a link, which I click without hesitation. It might be a glowing review or a harsh critique of my latest literary work. Nevil never takes the middle road.

I'm shocked to realise it's nothing like I expected. It's something else. Definitely something else.

"Big scoop from the publishing world. The rights to Markus Leigh's new novel have already been acquired for a film adaptation. There's already talk about a movie or perhaps a TV series!"

I recognise the publication, The Literary Scene, but... what on earth are they talking about? Probably The Black Shadows of Vengeance, obviously! But this isn't a real scoop; "Larsen Ink" was already negotiating to adapt my latest book. This news is from a few months ago.

In any case, I keep reading. And it feels as if the world suddenly collapsed onto me, along with all its weight.

"This time, it will be a troubled and painful love story, unlike Leigh's other novels, featuring family tragedies and unsettling twists. We talk about the author's very first book, set in the New England town of Salem Falls. Now we are all eager to

discover Markus Leigh from a more sentimental, intimate, and dramatic perspective, before his fame. Perhaps he's always concealed behind horror, but the truth is different. Are we ready to find out?"

Damn! No, no one's ready to find out. Especially not me!

I read the following lines, a sort of back cover of the work, with a growing concern that borders on anguish. They didn't mention the names, but... it's as if they did!

I feel like I'm sinking as I run both hands through my hair. Which book are they referring to? I haven't submitted anything else to "Larsen Ink". It can't be what I am afraid of, but they called it my very first book, so... There's no point in denying it; it truly is! It's obvious.

Damn, the novel where I shared part of my story with Caleb! There are even personal details. Too personal. Confidences only ours!

My hands are trembling as I ring Nevil. I feel nervous waiting for him to answer.

'Markus... How...'

I hardly even give him a chance to respond.

'Nevil, what on earth did you do? And more importantly... why?'

'Calm down, Markus, don't worry. I just shook things up a bit.' His tone is cheerful, almost euphoric. 'As they say... strike while the iron's hot!'

'But I hadn't yet...' I gasp, out of breath. I'm so nervous I can't carry on.

'I know, but we somewhat agreed. Anyway, I just sent a tantalising synopsis of your manuscript to a few magazines and blogs. And guess what? They loved it so much they can't wait to receive the finished novel! I know it still needs a proper ending, a revision from you, a thorough editing, and...'

'No, Nevil... you don't understand!'

He doesn't understand, and I feel like an idiot! What exactly did I promise him? Was it to publish that book? Yes, actually, I had considered it, mainly to avoid the pressure of having to start a new story. I agreed out of laziness and distraction, without really considering the content of that text! Only now do I see it clearly.

But... he should have warned me before sharing the plot of the story!

'I understand, Markus, I understand more than you think. And I assure you, this is a golden opportunity,' he sighs, and I imagine that, if I were standing in front of him, he would give me his typical condescending look, as if he were dealing with a stupid, unruly child. 'That novel is your chance for a drastic change in your career. I'd say you've grown quite a bit as a "promising young writer". It's time for a change of scenery. I mean... after this book, you could really write anything.'

There's no point in continuing to discuss it; he doesn't understand. Or rather, he doesn't care about understanding that I agreed out of boredom, recklessness, or because I was too distracted by Caleb, trying to mend our relationship, to think clearly about the matter.

I don't reply; I let him speak and then hang up. The damage is already done, and nothing would change. I just have to find a solution now.

I get up and step back to the window. The town is beginning to wake, illuminated by lanterns, autumn leaves, and vivid colours. But I feel overwhelmed, as if I've travelled a long way to come back here only to be crushed again by my own poor choices. It feels like I'm being pulled into quicksand, dragging me ever deeper without a chance to surface and breathe.

Caleb.

I know what's in that story. Us. Our first encounter, the bringing together of our destinies. An overwhelming, unstoppable love. And nothing has changed, because it still is that way. But there's so much more... the truth about our lives before Salem

Falls. Not so simple, not so exciting. Especially for him.

I can't wait any longer; I must go to him. I check the time, growing more impatient; "Moonlight" should be opening soon. I shower quickly, get dressed, and hurry to the shop.

When I walk in, I hope to find him behind the counter. I hope I can hold him back and speak to him before he finds out some other way. Above all, I hope he's not used to reading online magazines. I don't even know which other publication or blog Nevil "sold" that damned scoop to.

But Caleb isn't there. He's not behind the counter, nor in that part of the room I'm scanning. I glance around and see Chelsea appear, greeting me with a radiant smile. My expression must worry her, because hers also suddenly changes, her gaze darkening.

'Markus… is everything okay?'

'Yes, good.' There's no point worrying her. I don't have time to explain the situation. 'Is Caleb there?'

'Sure. He's in the back, sorting out some deliveries.' She nods doubtfully, glancing at me. 'More copies of your books have arrived, too, by popular demand! We ordered them with express shipping, so…'

I don't respond to her or even let her finish; I hurry over to him. There he is, with his shirtsleeves rolled up, leaning against the open space between the shelves, his phone in his hand. He's reading something, scrolling through it.

'Caleb, I... I need to talk to you.'

Just hearing my voice, he lifts his face towards me. His gaze is distant and cold, with his brow furrowed, as if there's nothing left of the boy I was with last night.

'About what, Markus?' He lifts his phone and angles the screen towards me. 'About this?'

Shit! This looks like the same article Nevil sent me.

'Caleb, you shouldn't have...'

'My aunt just sent it to me.' He sighs and shrugs. 'No problem, Markus. It just confirms that I was an idiot for... trusting you. For trying you, like you asked.'

'No, Caleb, that's not true.' I move quickly towards him, eager to seize him, hold him close, but his disgusted expression makes me hold back.

'You sold our story, Markus... You sold mine, more than anything! The abuse I endured as a child, my father's betrayals, my mother's suicide! Things I confided in you that you included in the drama of one of the characters in that novel you would never have published anyway! It was just... it was just ours...'

'No, I... I assure you it's not what it seems!'

'If it's not what it seems, how did they learn such details?' he sighs indignantly and shrugs. 'Did your publisher investigate my private life? My past? I really don't think so.'

'No, you're right. But I...'

I pause; any explanation I could offer would be incriminating. I had shared it with Nevil ten years ago for his second opinion on my writing, about a text that wasn't horror and which I believed was good. It was more challenging, deeper, and closer to what I aimed to achieve in the future. Yet, it would never be published.

Caleb shakes his head. He doesn't even seem angry with me now. Instead, he looks disappointed, and that hurts even more.

'Leave it, Markus. It doesn't matter.'

'No, it does. It matters, Caleb!'

'Okay... then explain. Is this what you were thinking when you came back here to Salem Falls? When you tried to get back together with me? When...' He widens his blue eyes at me. 'When did you want me to interview you? Was it when you fucked me last night? Were you already planning the marketing campaign for your new book? Wait, what did they write…' He glances at his mobile phone. 'Here it is: *'Markus Leigh from a more sentimental, intimate, and dramatic perspective, before his fame.'* And what was your drama? Not being appreciated enough by Mum and Dad? The competition with your sister? Nothing so terrible, after all, the real disasters happened to me and you thought it best to sell them. It's all part of a plan you put together with your publisher, right? That's what gave you the great idea of coming back to Salem Falls. You used me, Markus. You took advantage of me. Again!'

'No, Caleb.' His words cut more deeply than he realises. Each one wounds me like a blade, slicing deep. 'That's not true.'

He doesn't listen to me. He walks past me, leaves without looking back, and walks away. I'm left alone, feeling shocked and devastated. My hopes are shattered. It feels like I've truly lost him and that I'll never get the chance to recover.

Because if he never managed to hate me before, now… now he does.

Now he really hates me.

CHAPTER 12

Caleb

It's really over this time.

Even more than when he abandoned me ten years ago, without having the courage to look me in the face.

I don't even know what hurts more: anger or disappointment. I think it's disappointment, though. Even though I feel like I'm boiling.

How could he do something like this to me? Take advantage of me?

I let Chelsea take over the place for a moment and went up to my apartment to wait for Markus to leave. When I returned ten minutes later, he was gone. I couldn't even face him now.

It's as if my whole past, dating back to the years before Salem Falls, suddenly flooded back.

I had managed to rediscover myself, thanks to Aunt Leanne's care. I had exorcised part of my pain through theatre and Julia, who had taught me to regain my self-confidence by performing on stage. Then he, Markus, arrived, an unexpected love I hadn't been seeking. A love that helped heal my wounds, erase the guilt of being unable to defend myself from my father's business partner's abuse, and prevent my mother's suicide because of that man, who, besides refusing to believe my words, constantly cheated on her and treated her physically and psychologically with little mercy.

I know what people will uncover in that book. Not just my personal and family dramas, but also us, my rebirth thanks to Salem Falls, thanks to him. What we once were. Or, at least, what I fooled myself into thinking we could become together.

For ten years, sometimes without realising it, I searched for him in other people and relationships. I lived with the ghost of Markus haunting my mind and heart. Now that ghost has come back to reclaim my memories, wounds, and silences.

'Caleb...' Chelsea approaches, hesitating as she speaks. Her glance at me suggests she already knows everything. 'Markus explained it to me.'

'It's okay, Chelsea. He'll go away, and everything will go back to normal. Or at least I hope so.'

I hope I don't become a spectacle for inquisitive readers and Markus Leigh enthusiasts. A rather sad phenomenon to witness and possibly photograph to add to their collection of memorabilia about the great writer.

'Sure, but I think... you could sort it out. I'm sure there was a misunderstanding between him and his publisher, a nasty mistake, so...'

'It wasn't just a misunderstanding. I believe he and his publisher plotted it from the very start.'

She sighs and shakes her head. 'No, I don't think so. The publisher, perhaps, but not Markus. He was quite upset, Caleb.'

'Did you join his fan club, along with my aunt?' I huff in irritation, crossing my arms over my chest.

'No, I'm just trying to be as rational as I can.' She tilts her face, hinting at a sweet yet sad smile. 'I didn't even realise there was a relationship between you. I started to sense something, and then during the interview, it became even clearer.'

'It doesn't matter any more. There's nothing left between me and Markus.' I'm stern and uncompromising. I'm actually trying to convince myself more than her. But I notice my voice trembling. 'Now, excuse me, Chelsea. I don't want to talk about this any longer.'

I step outside "Moonlight" to finally end the conversation. I know Chelsea isn't the type of person who gives up so easily.

I'd like to leave, escape from here, at least for a while. But I can't leave Chelsea alone any longer; there are too many tourists in town and customers in the shop. I sigh, lower my gaze, and place a hand on my chest. I really need a break right now.

When I look up, I see Aunt Leanne staring at me suspiciously.

'Don't say anything, Aunt. I...'

'Caleb, you didn't mind that article, did you?'

I don't even know what to say to her. One way or another, she'll agree with Markus.

'It wouldn't make any difference, anyway,' I say, running a hand over my forehead. 'You don't know exactly what's in that book. I do. You can't understand...'

'I imagine so, though. Your story is in there, right?' Her voice remains calm and determined. Perhaps she doesn't realise how much of our personal stories have ended up in that manuscript.

'Ours... mine...' I lower my gaze. I don't want to dredge up the past, but I have to. 'You know what I mean, Aunt? I told Markus everything, in detail. And he got to work... so when I read it, written by him, it seemed less...'

My eyes are burning, and I bite my lips to hold back the tears.

'Less horrible?'

'No, perhaps not, in fact... it was even worse from that perspective. But it seemed to me that, for us, for me, it was possible to find some form of redemption... a bit of peace.'

Aunt Leanne nods and softly strokes my cheek.

'So he helped you through your grief, Caleb.'

'I know. But I trusted him! He shouldn't have exposed my story, about my mother, about my father who didn't care and immediately started a new life...' I look into her eyes, searching for a hint of anger, surrender, or weakness that I can't find in her. 'Can you accept it, Aunt?'

'Not always, dear. Your mother was my sister. We were twins, Caleb. Since she left, I haven't felt truly complete. But...' She closes her blue eyes for a moment, caressing my arms. 'But you came here, you chose this town, you decided to stay and build your life here again. And I know we have to move on. We owe it to her and to ourselves.'

'What Markus did was...'

'It was rubbish, really. And that's how you've got to see it.' She sighs, shrugging. 'It was careless of him. But I'm convinced he didn't mean you any harm.'

'Yes, maybe you're right,' I nod, forcing a smile. I don't want to talk about him any more. I decide to make use of my aunt's presence, since she knows the place at least as well as Chelsea and I do. 'Auntie, would you mind staying with Chelsea for a while? I need a break; I won't be gone long. I don't want to leave her alone.'

'Of course, dear, don't worry.'

I thank her and begin wandering aimlessly through the streets of Salem Falls. I can't tear myself away from him. I can't help but connect every emotion I have to Markus Leigh. Now, I feel condemned by my love for him.

I reach the harbour, the boats swaying gently in the distance. I sit on the dock and gaze out at the dark water. Meanwhile, I'm waging a battle with myself. Because there's a part of me that still justifies him, that wants to believe him. Then his voice resonates inside me, reminding me that he's never forgotten me. But perhaps, as he spoke those words, he was already thinking of using our story, my life, to sell me out. Maybe I should be proud of that, but I can't. I can't. Because I feel exposed, betrayed once again, traded for the dream of success that Markus has always sought.

My phone vibrates in my jacket pocket. I hear a text notification. I assume it's Chelsea or Aunt Leanne. They'll ask me to return, or perhaps they're simply worried about me. I've been gone for a while.

Instead, it isn't them.

"Please, let me explain. That wasn't what I intended. Can we talk?"

I close my eyes and I don't reply. Not now, at least.

Meanwhile, the rain begins to fall softly, like a veil. And, in the silence, I feel the only truth I have left emerge: the love that has never faded is also the one that hurts the most.

CHAPTER 13

Markus

I can't believe it has all started again and ended like this.

It isn't fair.

I don't deserve it. Not this time.

Maybe I should leave, but I stay here in Salem Falls. I can't move, nor can I convince myself to give up. I cling to the events planned for the Halloween festival and the writing workshops, where I try to share with children and adults some of what I have learned over the years. All of this is to reassure myself that staying isn't just about my own will. I hope little Daniel and the other participants don't pick up my mistakes along with my writing craft.

I don't understand how someone can feel both anger and grief at the same time, but for two days I've been living on this fragile edge. Soon I won't even have a formal reason to stay here in Salem

Falls. Halloween will be my downfall, and I'll be forced to leave. No trick-or-treating for me.

Meanwhile, Nevil's emails kept piling up, along with his calls and messages. He was understanding, stern, and sometimes even threatening.

To persuade me, he also forwarded the proposal they sent him for a movie based on my "still unnamed story".

All this fuss over a novel I don't want published. I feel trapped between "Larson Ink," the press releases, the interviews, the success, and the truth. And, above all this, there's him, Caleb. He who doesn't want to hear from me any longer.

My writing has been recognised as *"one of the most authentic voices on the contemporary scene."* Nevil was extremely proud of me and himself for discovering me, so he had that quote printed on the covers of numerous new editions of my books.

Now, I don't even know how to define myself. In many ways, perhaps. But not "authentic".

I look at myself in the mirror in my room at the Salem Falls Shelter: unkempt beard, increasingly dark circles under my eyes, more or less the same haggard appearance I had ten years ago when I left Salem Falls. But back then, I still had hope and enthusiasm in my eyes, even though I had been forced to give up so much.

Now I feel nothing but overwhelming exhaustion. Caleb's face, his words, and his disappointment in me linger in my mind, like an unhealable wound.

I can't carry on like this. I don't want to. I need to find a solution, and I have to be the one to do it; I can't wait for things to change on their own without my intervention.

I pick up the phone and decide to call Nevil back.

'Ah, finally!' His tone is halfway between relief and irony. 'Have you gotten over the blues, Markus?'

'No, I'd say not,' I reply firmly, nearly angry. He shouldn't have acted without my consent; he knows that too. 'In any case... Nevil, we need to talk.'

'I agree with that. Your novel could be the event of next year. There's been a huge buzz around that scoop; it was a brilliant idea! Many people are already waiting for it. Well, you can't ruin everything now.'

'Yes, indeed. That novel should never be published. You'll still need my approval for the "ready to print". Well, it might never happen.'

I am resolute and steadfast. I understand Nevil's tactics for persuading authors to accept even situations that, with a clear mind, might be deemed unacceptable. In practice, he is increasingly becoming a modern incarnation of his father, Clive Larsen, the notorious publishing shark.

He's still trying to go easy on me.

'Markus, as I have explained to you, it is already certain that it will be a bestseller. It will benefit everyone, I assure you. You can't...'

'Of course I can!' I interject. No, I won't get scammed again. 'Nevil, I see my contract with "Larsen Ink" is expiring soon, regarding several of my novels. I might not renew it or even terminate it before that happens.'

The silence that follows my statement is cold and stark, like ice. But Nevil quickly pulls himself together.

'Are you joking?'

'Not at all.' I refuse to give in; I won't let him frighten me. 'If that book gets published, I'll prove it to you with facts. So, if you want to test me...'

'Markus, may I remind you that all your success is due to "Larsen Ink"? That we supported and encouraged you from the very beginning, when no one else believed in you, step by step, over the past ten years?'

'Yes, and I thank you, Nevil.' I can't argue with that; he's right. 'I know that without you and "Larsen Ink", I would never have got anywhere. I owe you everything and will always be grateful.

But, at this point in my life, I'd rather lose what I've achieved than betray myself. And him.'

'Damn, Markus... how stubborn you are!'

Nevil sighs, and I begin to notice a sense of resignation in his tone, as if he is on the verge of surrendering. Maybe I am truly risking everything; maybe "Larsen Ink" will abandon me, leave me to my fate in favour of more relaxed, more accommodating, and more manipulable authors. Willing to accept any compromise. And I will lose everything I have gained over the years.

He doesn't say goodbye or farewell; he simply hangs up abruptly without saying anything further.

Alright, I think I've really pissed him off this time. Maybe this will truly be the end of my writing career.

I can hear the sound of my own laboured breathing, as if my body is struggling to contain the turmoil that is unleashing itself within me.

I start pacing my room, back and forth, like a lost soul.

I feel a thrill. I need... yes, perhaps I truly need to write. An almost visceral urge, like I haven't experienced in years. In fact, like I haven't felt since that summer when I decided to settle here in Salem Falls, indefinitely.

I grab my laptop and leave my room, heading down to the reception desk where I find Allie, who gives me an adoring look.

I decide to be polite and ask her if there's a spot in the hotel where I can write a bit and feel inspired by the atmosphere, maybe even have a coffee without being disturbed.

'Of course! There's the little veranda at the back. It's quite private and not very popular with our guests.' She smiles, seemingly pleased to be of assistance to my "art". She even shows more confidence, as if she's suddenly become a valuable ally in my writing. 'I can serve you coffee, some cakes... whatever you prefer.'

'Thank you, Allie. A ginseng coffee will do for now.'

I head to the back veranda she pointed out. She was right; it's free at the moment. I sit at one of the tables. Meanwhile, a waiter arrives with my coffee. I thank him and decide to get to work straight away. Or at least, I try.

I open my laptop.

Blank page. Blocked. Clouded mind.

Here we go, off to a good start! And yet, just a few minutes ago, everything seemed so clear to me!

Alright, I need to clear my mind if I want any hope of achieving anything.

I sip my coffee and scan the surroundings; the autumnal landscape, with its warm, rich, and deep colours, feels inspiring and reassuring. I close my eyes and take a deep breath. When I open them again, the blank page on my laptop remains before me. But I can do this now. I can face it.

So I start to write as I used to, without overthinking or aiming for perfection. I allow myself to be carried away by my emotions.

I write the first words without overthinking. I write from the heart, without even considering an ideal audience, as Nevil always taught me. I write for myself, perhaps. I write because I enjoy telling stories, regardless of whether anyone will ever read them or not.

"There were no monsters or ghosts that Halloween night. Just two young people who, after reuniting, were afraid to truly love each other, to transcend the darkness. They were afraid of their past, their present, and perhaps even their future. Until the real monsters reappeared once more in their lives, taking over their minds, hearts, and feeding on their fears, disappointments, and the loneliness that had overtaken their souls and taken root there."

My fingers move on their own. I'm not writing one of my usual horror novels, nor even a mystery.

I don't even know what the hell I'm writing. But I don't care, I keep going.

Perhaps, even if in a singular and contentious way, I am writing about us.

Of us, as we are now. Partly also of us, as we once were or could have been. Our hopes and dreams, cast to anyone willing to exploit a truth that burns inside me until it consumes me.

But, as far as I'm concerned, no gimmicks this time, no marketing or foolproof editorial strategies. Just love, in all its poetry, in all its imperfection.

The more I write, the more I feel the chains that have held me back breaking, especially over the past ten years.

I feel free now. I feel authentic.

This time I don't have an outline or a plan, even though ideas are flooding into my mind, unstoppable, meanwhile.

I don't even know how this story will end or what will happen to my characters. But it doesn't matter. Besides, I don't know what will happen to me tomorrow, in an hour, or even in five minutes.

I've never written this freely before. I've always planned everything carefully, including all the twists and turns. But this time, it's fine. I don't want to limit myself. The most important thing is to enjoy the story. The most important thing is to feel good.

Once I finish the first chapter, I take a deep breath. I feel as if I've been holding my breath while writing.

I stretch my shoulders, order another coffee, and begin to reread, more carefully, what I've written.

I like it. More than I expected, I'm pleased with my seven pages. And that's another strange thing, as far as I'm concerned. I'm almost never happy with my work.

I smile, feeling quite emotional, and bite my lip. Good... and now what am I supposed to do with this chapter?

It's quite clear, I'll do what I always do. I could start working on the second, the third, and so on...

I sigh, stroking my chin with my hand; my beard feels more bristly than usual.

Maybe I should... but no, that seems absurd to me! Although, after all... why not?

I access the Salem Falls Festival's writing workshop platform, which is open to provide students with further guidance and the opportunity to publish their work online, even in serial form, and have it judged directly by readers.

After the hours I spent teaching at the workshop, I hadn't considered the idea of people publishing their writing on the "Salem Falls Writing Lab".

Clearly, that didn't interest me at the time, except to inspire some writing.

But what can I do now? Alright, that would be silly. I'm an established writer; I don't need this gimmick to attract readers.

But I'm curious; the thought of putting myself out there as if I were a beginner tempts me... and then...

Well, yes, I want to try! I register, log in to the site, and upload my chapter. I need a cover image; from where I am, I take a photo with my phone, a tree-lined avenue visible from the back of "Salem Falls Shelter". In any case, no one would connect this image to me. Also, no one would expect me to publish on that platform.

But I can't use my real name, that's for certain; I need to think of a pseudonym or a fitting nickname.

I think about it for a few minutes before choosing the perfect name. One that no one could associate with me. Almost no one.

Then I click "submit publication", and my chapter of the story, tentatively titled *Beyond the Darkness*, goes online.

I sigh and keep my gaze fixed on the website page, or rather, on my recently published work. I feel an unusual emotion, one I can't quite explain. If Nevil knew, he'd give me a proper telling off. I feel like a rebellious kid who disobeys the rules. Besides, I shouldn't publish anything without my publisher's consent. Least of all, a chapter of an unpublished story on the website of a writing workshop for new and beginning writers.

I close my laptop, deciding to forget what I've written and the publication of the first chapter, and lose myself in observing the landscape around me. I need some peace. It was a foolish thing on my part, clearly. However, at least for a few hours, I managed to disconnect, free myself from my thoughts and my troubles. I felt relieved, almost invigorated.

I get up, stretch, maybe go for a walk. I'd like to go back to "Moonlight" and try to clear things up with Caleb. But I'm afraid I'll make the situation worse.

In the meantime, I'll take my laptop back to my room. Maybe later I'll return to working on the second chapter of this entirely unplanned story, with more coffee.

I hardly step off the porch when I hear a notification on my phone. I check it; it's from the "Salem Falls Writing Lab".

I can't believe there's already a comment on my chapter! I'm so curious, I'm heading to my page now to check.

"I don't know you, but this story really moved me, in a good way. Well done, White Nights."

The commenter remains anonymous, but it doesn't really matter. He doesn't realise it, but White Nights is me! Damn, I feel as excited as a child starting out. I could be the same age as Daniel right now!

I smile. Not so much for the compliment, but because I'm beginning to feel alive again.

I rush up to my room and dial Nevil's number. He's still mad at me, obviously. If he knew what I'd done, he'd kick me out of "Larsen Ink" in a heartbeat. Now, however, he's "simply" threatening to sue me, claiming that everything I write belongs to the publishing house. And if it's a manuscript I gave him myself, I haven't got a chance of winning.

'I understand, Nevil. What if we reach an agreement?'

'What agreement?'

'I give you everything — all the rights to the novels I've published over the years with "Larsen Ink", and whatever comes from them: movies, TV series, video games... You can have them forever without owing me anything. Of all my novels, except that one.'

He mutters some insults, of which I can clearly hear only "you damn stubborn asshole", then hangs up.

Perhaps he's considering it. Or perhaps he's beginning to realise that this is a genuinely critical issue for me, not just a whim.

I sigh and look out the window. Salem Falls is bathed in a morning of increasingly vivid, coppery autumn colours. Maybe I'm sinking; my career as a recognised writer is really at risk of collapsing. But I don't care.

Because, for the first time in ages, I don't feel oppressed. I want to work again, to live. Above all, I want to pick up my laptop and write the second chapter of a story that I don't yet know where it will lead, but which finally allows me to breathe and hope for a happy ending.

CHAPTER 14

Caleb

I don't want to see Markus any longer. I don't want to hear about him any longer.

I don't mind if he insists on staying here in Salem Falls. He's just wasting his time.

That's what I tell myself while making another morning coffee. Meanwhile, Chelsea chats with the customers, and Aunt Leanne, as soon as she arrived at "Moonlight", convinced me to read some stories published on the "Salem Falls Writing Lab" website. After years, she's decided to join the organising committee and promised to take charge. The platform has been opened to writing workshop students, and readers are encouraged to leave comments, just to liven things up and motivate the authors.

'They need it. I've written down what I believe are the best. I can't review them; I must remain impartial.'

'All right, Aunt. I'll try to have a look when I get a break.'

'There's one in particular you absolutely must read!' When she becomes this insistent, there's no escape. I'm bound to give in and obey, or she'll keep pestering me. 'A new author, his nickname is White Nights, just published it. It's only the first chapter, but I assure you it's very promising.'

I was compelled to read and follow her instructions. I recognise that her intentions were good, but I did not voice my opinion on the matter; I kept my thoughts to myself. And for White Nights.

'So, what do you think?' she asked as soon as he noticed me putting my phone away. I saw she was watching me the whole time, waiting for my reaction.

'Not bad.' I know what she's expecting, but I prefer not to reveal too much. 'I'll continue with the other stories this evening.'

I don't feel particularly motivated to engage with other fame-hunting writers at the moment, but these poor fellows certainly aren't to blame for my unresolved feelings towards the great Markus Leigh. And besides, I run a café-bookshop, so I am compelled to interact with writers, whether I like it or not.

My real problem is that every time I hear his name, my stomach clenches. He's still here. And people talk about him, of course. So, I feel like a Grinch, but instead of hating Christmas, I hate Halloween. Luckily, it will all be over soon. The tourists who came specifically to celebrate Halloween will go home; the frenzy will pass, and Salem Falls will return to its usual quietness.

Nevertheless, I'm busy at my shop, doing my best. Working is one of the few things that keeps me going. It's what kept me going when he left the first time. Now I just have to wait for him to do it again; I can't expect him to decide to stay here in Salem Falls indefinitely.

When I retreat to my apartment above the shop, I relax on the sofa and use my phone to access the "Salem Falls Writing Lab" platform. I notice almost immediately that the first story Aunt Leanne recommended has been updated. Nearly all of them are set during this time of year, but this one... this one feels truly special, actually. I still can't quite work out where White Nights is heading, and it piques my curiosity. Moreover... it's almost as if it's speaking about me. Or rather, as if it's addressed directly to me, to be honest.

Without hesitation, I immerse myself in reading the second chapter of *Beyond the Darkness*. I follow the adventures of the two main characters with interest, until one sentence in particular strikes me deeply.

'We deceived ourselves into thinking we were hunting monsters, but in truth we were starting to realise that the real monsters were within us, concealed behind the masks of mistrust and pride.'

I swallow with difficulty, feeling my throat tighten. I decide to carry on, but it's as if each sentence is a fragment of my story, of the fear of losing myself that has always gripped my heart.

I'm also rereading the first chapter, which had already affected me this morning. Now it affects me a second time, even more profoundly.

And the initial suspicion I worked so hard to dismiss is starting to be confirmed. It's not a coincidence. It's him. White Nights. The first book he recommended to me, almost as a joke, when we first met. That's why Aunt Leanne encouraged me to read the stories posted on the site, including this one. She must have recognised his style quite easily. But she knew that if she had told me from the start that it was Markus, I would have refused to read it, as I've always done with his books, after all.

It's him, but not as he has become now. Between these sentences, he appears vulnerable. Fragile. Yet he's genuine. His writing isn't as intricate as it has been recently, but it lacks the brashness and irreverence it had at the start of his career. And now, in every word, I notice a tenderness I once thought was lost, gone forever.

I continue to read and reread, several times, even slowly, almost fearfully. Then I close the site, turn off my mobile phone, and remain silent. I can only hear the pounding of my heart.

I close my eyes and lean my head against the backrest, trying to relax. When I open them again, I realise I have been asleep for about two hours.

I pick up my phone again; I can't help myself. I log back into the site and see that White Nights has published yet another chapter.

I try to resist, to think of something else, but I can't help it. I immerse myself in my reading once again. One of the characters in the story utters these words:

'Sometimes love doesn't die, but chooses to remain silent. It waits for someone to find the courage to return and build a new world. Sometimes you need to walk through darkness to reach the light.'

I miss him. Honestly, I've always missed him more than I've ever dared to admit. I still miss him desperately.

And it's not a question of whether I forgive him for exposing our private life in a novel his publisher will publish. I try to be honest, at least with myself. That was just an excuse, a pretext. The truth is, I'm afraid—the same fear I had ten years ago, when I let him go without a fight. Now I'm terrified of having him back only to lose him again. That's why I resist the temptation to run to him, to hug him, to confess my feelings, to ask him to stay with me. That's why I continue to live in a state of uncertainty, caught between anger and regret.

I'm rereading the chapters of his new story, published on a platform designed for emerging writers, once again. I'm reaching the third chapter and, beneath those of other readers, I'm adding my new comment, choosing to remain anonymous, just like I did with the first.

Just a few words.

"I'll wait for you."

I'm anonymous, like many others. I didn't choose a nickname that reveals my identity. It doesn't matter if he understands it, honestly, but I can no longer escape or even pretend to myself.

Markus doesn't know it's me.

Or perhaps he will understand.

Whatever the situation, what matters to me is that, on the other side of the screen, he knows I am listening. The silence between us will never be a closed door, but perhaps just a pause, like the one I am experiencing now.

A painful, fragile, yet vital pause… as I await the next chapter.

CHAPTER 15

Markus

I haven't slept for two nights. I'm a mess. I'm in really poor shape, with a greenish complexion and dark circles under my eyes that are becoming darker and deeper. Essentially, I'm turning into a living Halloween mask. Not even when I reach the final chapters of my novels or Nevil is pressing me to meet deadlines do I look this bad.

Despite everything, I completed the writing workshop, handed out the various diplomas to the students, and did my best for those who entrusted me here in Salem Falls. It was a wonderful experience for me, and I hope to do it again someday.

But since I read that cryptic comment, *"I'll wait for you"*, my mind has offered no respite.

I know it's him. I feel it in every fibre of my being. I hear his voice, I can even sense his gaze, between my words and his, behind the screen that separates us. I've written three more chapters of the new story, but I haven't published them yet. I fear his judgment, I confess.

It's Halloween. I walk through the crowd with my hood pulled over my head, trying to blend my heartbeat with that of the world around me, which at this moment feels like an unstoppable carousel of masks and colours. Kids dressed as vampires and witches run through the alleys, trying to gather as many sweets as possible, the lights flicker on the windows, and the air smells of sugar and hot chocolate. But inside me, there's only silence, just now. Only him.

I draw closer and closer, walking around the "Moonlight" along parallel paths, gazing at it from a distance without summoning the courage to enter.

What if I misunderstood his request?

I'm too frightened he'll reject me again. But I can't wait any longer, and I've realised the situation could stay like this forever if I don't do something to change it. So, I must act.

A gentle but stealthy drizzle falls as I pass by the windows of the "Moonlight Café & Bookshop". I catch a glimpse of Chelsea just as she, too, looks outside. She gazes at me intently for a moment, then nods for me to come in.

I seize the opportunity, approach, and take a deep breath as I pass through the entrance to "Moonlight". I am immediately greeted by the scent of vanilla, cookies, and coffee that I associate with Caleb's place. Besides Chelsea, there's a tall, blond man behind the counter. But it's not him. I recognise him; it's Chelsea's boyfriend.

'Hi,' Chelsea greets me with a slight smile.

'Hi.' No need to waste time with pleasantries; I want to get straight to the point. I want to see him. 'Is he here?'

'No, he went to pick up Julia from the airport, along with Leanne. You know she always comes back for Halloween. But they're arriving soon; they'll be here any minute. Steve stayed to give me a hand.' She tilts her head, strokes my arm, perhaps to comfort me. Then she gestures towards one of the empty tables. 'Take a seat. Would you like a coffee? Ginseng as usual?'

'Yes, please.'

I nod and sit at the table. I try hard to calm down, but... damn, my hands are trembling! Chelsea serves me my coffee, but I still can't relax. I feel like I'm about to sit an exam... actually, no. Much worse!

After about ten minutes, the door opens with its usual chime, and the orange pumpkin overhead casts a glow. Now, a faintly sadistic, witch-like laugh accompanies the light.

I bite my lip, waiting for the person who opened the door to step through the entrance.

It's him.

Caleb walks in with his jacket hood wet and his blond hair tousled. His beard looks a little longer than usual. As he moves towards the centre of the room, his eyes lock onto me. For a moment, I feel as if the entire universe suddenly comes to a halt.

I remain silent, waiting. We gaze at each other for what seems like an eternity, then he decides to come over to my table.

But he remains still and keeps looking at me, not sitting opposite. So I decide to speak first.

'Thanks for reading my story.' I sigh, biting my lip. 'Those three chapters, I mean.'

He nods and shrugs.

'I didn't know it was yours initially.'

Maybe I started at the wrong point, but it doesn't matter. I know exactly where I want to go.

'Okay, anyway. I'm not here for that, I... I'm here for you.'

Caleb remains standing, crossing his arms over his chest. He does not reply, but he does not step back.

So, after taking a deep breath, I decide to carry on. And I get up as well.

'You have every right to hate me, Caleb. I was wrong. I let my career become more important than what truly mattered: the two of us.' My heart pounds, and I feel a lump in my throat that nearly chokes me. I can't lose him again. I don't want to. 'I let Nevil use private details of our lives, especially yours, our relationship, because I foolishly passed that manuscript to him years ago. But it wasn't intended for publication, it never was. By the time he acted, as you know… it was already too late. And anyway, I had agreed, without thinking, because… I was too nervous at the thought of having you by my side again, after our interview…'

'Markus…'

'No, let me finish. Listen to me, Caleb, please. I swear I didn't mean to harm you or deceive you. I didn't mean to hurt you again.'

His expression remains impassive, but his blue eyes show a flicker of emotion. I then seize this opportunity to continue.

'When I realised what was happening… I asked Nevil to put everything on hold. I lost my contracts, the publisher's trust. Maybe I'll lose the other books too. I don't know, and honestly, I don't even care.

The only thing that really matters to me is not losing you… again. And if you ask me to wait, I'll wait.' My voice cracks; I need his answer now, whatever it is. 'I love you, Caleb. Always have. But if it's right for you to never see me again, I'll accept that. If you ask me to leave Salem Falls once and for all, I'll leave. I just want you to know that my love has never been a lie, and that I… never thought I'd take advantage of you to sell our story.'

Caleb sighs but stays silent, his eyes still fixed on me. Then he slightly shakes his head and lowers his gaze.

When he looks back at me, I notice his eyes are shining.

'Caleb…'

'I'm sorry, Markus. I'm sorry, but I can't.'

CHAPTER 16

Caleb

I can't.

I can't get him out of my mind. I can't forget him either.

There are many things I can't do.

But for now, I can only let him go when, upon hearing my words, I see him startle, lower his eyes, and then walk towards the entrance to leave the shop.

A few moments later, Aunt Leanne and Julia enter and give me a puzzled look.

'Caleb... What did you do?' My aunt rushes over, catches up with me, and looks at me sternly. 'We saw Markus leave, and... he didn't even stop.'

'You sent him away.' Julia follows her, and they both stand facing me.

Julia's isn't a question; our drama teacher immediately understood what had happened, even without witnessing the scene. She sighs and shakes her head, letting her red curls sway over her shoulders.

'It wasn't supposed to end like this!' Chelsea intervenes, of course. 'But why?'

What precisely is it? An encirclement?

Why did it end like this?

Why did I send him away?

Yes, Markus took my words as a farewell. And indeed, I can't fault him this time.

I bite my lip hard, feeling myself shivering and, at the same time, feeling cold inside. In my gut, in my bones.

From the window of "Moonlight", I look out.

It's Halloween. Of course, we couldn't have picked a better day, even if we wanted to, for a clarification or whatever it is.

Either way, I just want to vanish now, blend into the crowd among the masks, pumpkin jack-o'-lanterns, trick-or-treaters, and the orange and gold lights that adorn the streets of downtown Salem Falls.

I glance innocently at the three accusing women before me, then walk towards the entrance and cross the threshold. The little witch that Chelsea added this morning is cackling sadistically. She doesn't always behave that way with everyone, but she must have been particularly vicious about me! It almost seems as if they've set her on me. I wouldn't be surprised!

I find myself outside "Moonlight". The voices from the Halloween parade blend into a hum of music, drums, and laughter.

I glance both ways and see him standing nearby, his back against the wall and staring into space.

I remain still for a few moments before deciding to reach out to him. My mind and heart constantly search for him; this is my true challenge. His name burns inside me like a flame that never goes out, even in the storm.

I stand before him, and he remains motionless, his gaze unfocused, even though I am now the one filling the empty space that was just in front of him a moment ago. Suddenly, I feel as if I am returning to that summer when everything began. But this man before me is no longer the boy I lost ten years ago.

For a moment, all the noise around us seems to fade into complete silence. As if my world is holding its breath to utter a single name: his.

'You know what's the worst part, Markus?' His dark eyes widen slightly, but I don't give him time to answer. 'That I believe you.'

'Then why…' he barely whispers, his voice low, as if every word pains him.

'Because believing you isn't enough for me. Just as loving someone isn't enough to heal the wounds. Because it still hurts. But...'

I don't know what to do or how to move forward. Am I truly ready to let him go, to lose him forever? To never see him again?

He encourages me to continue.

'Go on, Caleb, please. I can handle anything.'

'But that new story of yours, your words... I've read and reread them so many times over the last few hours.'

'Really?'

'Yes, every word. Every damn line!' I nod, no longer hesitating. 'And, perhaps for the first time, I felt like I was hearing your voice. The real one, the one I loved and that spoke only to me, to my heart. Not the one you used ten years ago to try to impress publishers, not the one in your most famous novels... Not even the voice of that painful and too personal story we shared as we tried to overcome the pain. But yours, Markus. Yours. And it was like reading inside me. Because... as you wrote... *Sometimes you need to walk through darkness to reach the light.*'

I see tears welling up in his eyes, which suddenly become brighter and more intense than ever.

'And... so?'

'So I don't know, not yet. I only know I don't want to run away any longer. I can't if my heart remains stuck in the same place.'

As the festive lights around us seem to cast golden reflections on his handsome face, Markus offers a subtle smile, still shy and hesitant. His eyes now sparkle with gentle surrender, perhaps hope. And I feel something breaking and then coming together inside me.

He raises his hand and extends it towards me. I nod and brush it with my own, then bend it slightly to interlock my fingers with his. I close my eyes for a moment, letting his warmth flow through my skin.

'Alright, Caleb. That's fine.'

Meanwhile, the festival continues, unaware that two people are reconnecting after years of stubborn silence, caused by misunderstandings that nearly broke their hearts again.

'That's fine.' As I repeat his words, I gently touch his face with my other hand, damp with that persistent light rain, or perhaps with tears. 'I never stopped loving you, Markus.'

I take another step towards him, bring my face close to his, and kiss him on the lips. Meanwhile, time seems to stand still once more, and Salem Falls, with its ghosts of the past, shadows, and eternal legends, begins to breathe again around us.

But in this moment, so unique, so unrepeatable and precious, there are no more shadows between Markus and me. Only us and our love, which finally has the flavour of rebirth.

EPILOGUE

Three months later

Markus

Dawn light filters through the windows of "Moonlight", casting golden arabesques on the wooden tables and brightly decorated cups. Salem Falls always feels like a different town when the streets aren't overrun with lanterns, pumpkins, and Halloween costumes. The wind is colder, the sky darker, but my life, since that October 31st of last year, has been wonderfully sunny and clear.

I like to start early, well before the shop opens. The bell on the door, the only Halloween remnant we've decided to keep, remains silent, the counter is spotless, and the aroma of coffee floats in the air like a gentle touch. It has become my routine now. I enjoy writing here at "Moonlight", and no one is surprised anymore to see a 'famous' writer in Salem Falls.

Three months have gone by since the day we truly met again and still, when I close my eyes, I can taste the kiss with which Caleb welcomed me back into his life.

Now my home is here, with him. The place I always wanted to be. The place I should have stayed.

I sit at the corner table, the one I usually take, and turn on my laptop. I keep writing, despite everything. Because I love it, I love creating stories, not for success or recognition.

My fingers move slowly, and the sentences come effortlessly. I reread them, savouring every syllable. I've reached the final chapters of the story that has allowed me to regain a place in Caleb's heart. *Beyond the darkness.* I feel a profound emotion flowing through me.

It's not just a story of monsters; above all, it's a story of real, imperfect people who find the strength to move forward and face their fears and weaknesses.

I hear footsteps behind me. Caleb has just come down from the apartment we now share on the upper floor of "Moonlight". He approaches with two cups of ginseng coffee and hands me one, sitting down at the other end of the table.

'You've been awake for hours, haven't you? I didn't even hear you.'

He looks at me suspiciously. I know it by now, there's no point in denying it.

'The truth is, I hardly slept. In fact, almost none. You know... I want to finish it today!'

'You said that yesterday as well, Markus.'

'In fact, since I didn't sleep... technically, it's still yesterday for me!'

I chuckle and bite my lip, intentionally teasing. He sighs and rolls his eyes.

'You're so stubborn, you'll get there.'

'Thank you for your trust!' I wink at him and reach out to take his hand.

'But you need to rest, at least a little.'

'I promise I will... in fact, maybe we'll go somewhere! I want to celebrate!' I'm excited by the idea. 'But this story now needs a fitting ending. It won't be easy.'

'And then? Have you decided what you'll do with it?'

'No, not yet.'

I don't want to revert to the same situation that tore us apart ten years ago. At this stage, I'd rather put this story away and forget about it forever.

'You should send it to Nevil…'

Caleb's suggestion doesn't surprise me. He knows that "Larsen Ink Publishing" is willing to continue working with me, even though I stopped Nevil from publishing the unpublished novel I sent him years ago. And I know that my publisher has finally understood my intentions. But...

'I'm not sure,' I decide to be honest with him. I've always been since we chose to give each other a second chance. 'I don't want to ruin everything again, that's all.'

'It won't happen, don't worry.'

He seems exceptionally confident. While I appreciate his trust in me, I also fear that something beyond our control might once again disturb the relationship we are rebuilding together.

'Okay, I'll think about it.' I try to delay making the decision, at least for now.

'Markus… *Sometimes you need to walk through darkness to reach the light.*' Do you agree?'

'Yes, of course.'

I'm not sure what he's implying. But maybe, knowing him, I have a rough idea.

'Then give it a go. Send your story to Nevil. You deserve your success, now more than ever.'

'But, I...' I sigh, running a hand through my hair. 'Caleb, I don't want to risk losing you again, that's all!'

'Everything's going to be fine, Markus. You won't lose me.' He smiles, squeezes my hand, and intertwines his fingers with mine. 'I trust you.'

Three more months later

Caleb

I had no choice but to persuade him to get his life back, because it was the right thing to do. It's always been the right thing for him.

Markus is a writer. He's also many other things, but writing and storytelling are his passions. I cannot and will not take that away from him because what he writes deserves to be read and appreciated by many. That's why I persuaded him to send his new novel to Nevil.

Much has changed over the past ten years. We have changed as well.

For too long, I have built walls around myself. Between me and Markus, between me and what I have lost, between me and my pain, and between me and life itself. I wrongly believed that this would protect me. However, I was mistaken; it was simply the most effective way to hurt myself.

Now we pursue our projects bravely, one after the other. We share ideas often, and sometimes argue passionately. But we always try to be honest with each other, even if we don't always agree. We have realised that, as far as we're concerned, it's the only way we can stay together.

In these times, I realise that the perfect happiness I naively hoped for many years ago doesn't exist. Only fragments of peace, like the one we're experiencing right now.

"Sometimes you need to walk through darkness to reach the light."

It's more than just a sentence. It's the culmination of everything Markus and I have experienced.

Because that's simply how we are—two imperfect souls who have found their perfection together again.

The shadows were us, our silences, and our fear of being hurt again. But the light... well, the light is what we discovered together, dropping our masks and letting go of our pride.

It all happened thanks to the support of the people who have been close to us over the past few weeks, encouraging us to reconnect. And also thanks to the "Calloway Theatre", where our love blossomed and then revived to shine once more.

That's why we immediately realised we couldn't let it go.

With Julia Calloway's approval and the support of the Salem Falls Events Committee, we immediately began renovating the theatre. Some of the work is still ongoing, but we managed to reopen it for a few readings, with Julia herself participating as a guest speaker.

The walls still show signs of age, but the stage now hosts small events, and Julia, especially with Markus's help, will soon resume some of her acting classes. In short, we've persuaded her to return and get going again.

It's as if this place aims to complete a cycle, returning what we had lost, and then starting a new one. Now, this theatre, perhaps because it has finally regained nearly its former popularity, radiates a warmth that makes it feel alive, reborn, emerging from the ashes of a past that struggled to be present once again.

In fact, the reading cycles, which have become a vital part of our project, were introduced to prepare for the event that will take place on the occasion of the publication of Markus Leigh's new book.

Now, it's a world premiere that Markus and I will present together here at the "Calloway Theatre". Although he wasn't exactly too pleased with the idea I shared with Aunt Leanne and Chelsea, which also involved Nevil Larsen. Yes, because Nevil was so eager about Markus's new work that he's scheduled the publication and distribution of *Beyond the Darkness* within the next six months. He's organising a big event for Halloween here in Salem Falls. He even admitted it was a wise decision not to publish Markus Leigh's first story if he could get this one in instead.

'I think this theatre wanted to give us a second chance that night.' Thinking back about six months, the words come naturally. 'Halloween and the "cover of darkness" during the blackout did the rest.'

Markus smiles and nods. 'Maybe it's not just the "Calloway Theatre"; it's the town of Salem Falls itself that harbours a fondness for tormented souls.'

'Sure, then I'd say we're in the right place.'

I laugh and stroke his back. He's truly handsome, his dark eyes reflecting the energy and passion he feels as he talks about his new story. After all, this is his night.

Markus seizes the chance to steal a kiss from me, brushing his hand against my side.

'Don't give me any strange ideas; we are right at the same spot we were that evening!'

Our enthusiasm is instantly dampened by Chelsea, who approaches us with a worried yet euphoric expression.

'Are you guys ready? The audience is almost full!'

'Yes, I'd say so!' I nod confidently.

'No, I'd say not at all!' Markus replies, shaking his head. 'Didn't people really have anything better to do this evening?'

'Apparently not!' I smile and wink. 'They all want to see you and learn more about your masterpiece.'

'Oh, thanks. Now I feel truly relaxed!'

'Want to relax even more? Aunt Leanne texted me to let us know your parents and sister are here.'

'Then just clearly say that you want to kill me!'

'I want to kill you, Markus.' It's better if he knows. It won't change anything, but I'd like him to feel proud of himself and his work. 'In the front row, besides Nevil, there's also Clive Larsen, your big boss! And you know he never leaves his empire. Of course, I think he also did it to see Julia... but meanwhile, he's here!'

'Thanks, dear. Do you have a stake hidden in your jacket that you can stick in my heart?'

'I can always get it if you become a vampire! But considering your schedule... maybe you're on the right track!'

'No, Caleb... Vampires don't drink ginseng coffee!'

'I don't know; I should look into it...'

Chelsea seems satisfied with our way of communicating, which also shows how we are most of the time.

'Perfect! Keep it up throughout the interview and you'll be a hit!' she giggles. 'Like last time, people love your banter! It'll be a hit!'

I sigh and roll my eyes. We always joke about it, but the truth is that everything we've been through, the silences, the anger, the separation, has brought us to this point. Our relationship now isn't perfect, and maybe it never will be, but it's real.

As Chelsea walks onto the stage to introduce us to the audience, I shake Markus's hand behind the curtain.

'By now, after so many years, I've become accustomed to giving presentations, but... this book stands apart from all the others I've written.' He looks at me with a flicker in his eyes that touches me, genuinely moves me. 'This one has a truly happy ending. One I've never managed to craft in any other book. Mine. My happy ending.'

'I know, honey. Don't worry.' I gently touch his cheek with my fingers as Chelsea calls out our names. 'In fact, show your emotion, Markus. It's the best part of you.'

It's our moment. We leave the wing and step onto the stage of the "Calloway Theatre" to face our evening together.

Now, after so much time, I no longer fear the shadows beside Markus. I know there will still be some crossing our path, but we will face them together. And we will be able to be a light for each other, to confront whatever darkness fate throws at us.

Just like that sentence in the third chapter of Markus's book that marked our turning point and became our mantra.

"Sometimes you need to walk through darkness to reach the light."

About the author:

Facebook: https://www.facebook.com/justicewilloughbyauthor

Instagram: https://www.instagram.com/justicewilloughbyauthor

www.ingramcontent.com/pod-product-compliance
Lightning Source LLC
Chambersburg PA
CBHW052132170626
46812CB00004B/1378